THE FIGHT FOR
TRUTH

JEDI APPRENTICE

STAR WARS®

JEDI APPRENTICE

The Fight for Truth

Jude Watson

LUCAS
BOOKS

SCHOLASTIC INC.

New York Toronto London Auckland Sydney
Mexico City New Delhi Hong Kong

ISBN 0-590-52080-6

12 11 10 9 8 7 6 5 4 3 2 1   0 1 2 3 4 5 6/0

Printed in the U.S.A.
First Scholastic printing, August 2000

CHAPTER 1

The darkness was total. Not even a hint of light penetrated the hood. Sound was muffled. Obi-Wan Kenobi balanced on his feet, kept his lightsaber in a defensive position, and concentrated. Without sight or clear sound, he had to rely completely on the Force.

He moved to the left, whirled, and struck with his lightsaber. It slashed through empty air. Yet he knew he'd been close.

Off to his right, he heard a buzzing sound, and the clatter of metal hitting the floor.

"Point, Siri," Obi-Wan's Master, Qui-Gon Jinn, said quietly.

Obi-Wan felt a trickle of sweat move down his neck. The hood was hot from his warm breath. He gripped his lightsaber harder. His opponent in this training exercise was Siri, another Jedi apprentice. She had already destroyed two seeker droids. He hadn't felled one.

"Remember your purpose, Obi-Wan."

He heard Qui-Gon's steady counsel. Even though Qui-Gon couldn't see his Padawan's face, he knew that Obi-Wan had lost his focus. The purpose of the exercise, Obi-Wan knew, was cooperation. It did not matter how many seeker droids he destroyed or how many were taken down by Siri. They would be judged on how they worked together. They would have to read each other's intentions through movement, instinct, and the Force. They would have to be generous, reaching out to each other to reveal their intentions.

But how could he reach out to someone who fought only for herself?

Siri focused on the enemy and ignored Obi-Wan. A skilled, graceful fighter, she was single-minded in her purpose. Every particle of her being was focused on victory. It made her one of the best lightsaber fighters in the Temple. Even though she was eleven — two years younger than Obi-Wan — she had fought in his classes.

Faintly, he heard Siri's soft footsteps behind him, and heard her foot slide as she lunged. Another buzz, another clatter of metal.

"Good footwork, Siri," Adi Gallia called.

Obi-Wan gritted his teeth. Adi had only recently taken Siri as her Padawan. She had chosen Siri because of the girl's extraordinary promise. Now Siri was proving her value, showing up a more experienced Padawan — Obi-Wan.

Frustration and irritation surged inside him, driving out his connection to the Force. Obi-Wan listened intently for the slight stir in the air that the seeker droid caused. He heard the sound, whirled to his left, and collided with Siri.

"Opposite corners," Adi rapped out. "Begin again."

Obi-Wan moved back to his corner. He rubbed his palm along his tunic. His hands were perspiring, and his lightsaber almost slipped. Dropping it while fighting alongside Siri would be humiliating.

He wished he had Qui-Gon's patience. He still had so much to learn. Try as he might, he could not penetrate Siri's devotion to the exercise. It was *her* battle, *her* challenge. There was no room for him.

They started forward again. Obi-Wan moved slowly, reaching out to the Force to tell him where the seeker droids were flying. He heard another *clang* as a seeker droid hit the floor.

"Trust your partner as well as the Force," Adi called. "Aggression and competitiveness have no place in this exercise."

Obi-Wan felt Siri move slightly nearer to him.

Yet he still felt nothing from her. Another seeker droid hit the floor, and Obi-Wan's irritation crested and drove out his caution. He reached out, ignoring Siri.

Buzz, clang! A seeker droid hit the floor as he dropped to one knee and made a horizontal sweep. He rolled to his left, then swung upward. *Clang!* Another droid hit the floor. Why should he wait for Siri's cooperation while she destroyed all the droids herself? He would look like a fool.

Obi-Wan twisted, lunged, and attacked again. He heard Siri's breathing and the whisper of her quick footwork as she did the same. Within minutes, the two of them had destroyed every seeker droid in the room.

Obi-Wan felt a glow of satisfaction as he removed his hood. They had defeated their opponents in record time. Siri threw back her hood and pushed her golden hair behind her ears. Her vivid blue eyes blazed with satisfaction. They bowed to each other, then turned to face their Masters.

"You have both failed the exercise," Qui-Gon said sternly.

Adi rose, her garments rustling. Her tall stature and air of command made her an intimidating figure. She drew Siri aside and began to speak to her in a low tone. Qui-Gon tossed a towel to Obi-Wan so that he could wipe the perspiration off his forehead.

"I know you can fight," Qui-Gon told him. "You've proven yourself in battle after battle. That was not the point of the exercise, Padawan."

"I know," Obi-Wan admitted. "But she —"

Qui-Gon didn't wait for him to finish. "Siri has her own strengths and weaknesses. That was for you to discover. You merge with the strength, cover the weakness. Together, the two of you are stronger."

"Siri did no better than I did," Obi-Wan said. He knew he sounded sulky, but he couldn't help himself. It was Siri who had changed the rules of the exercise.

"Siri is not my Padawan," Qui-Gon said sternly. "We are speaking of you. Remember, Obi-Wan, the fear of looking like a fool is never a reason to do something. Or not do it. It is a fear born in weakness."

Obi-Wan nodded. He knew better than to continue to challenge Qui-Gon. At least they would soon be leaving. He would not have to repeat the exercise with Siri. Yoda had informed them that he was sending them on a mission.

Just then Yoda entered the training room. He

tucked his hands inside his robe, waiting for them to face him.

"A summons we have received," he said. "Parents have contacted the Jedi. Think they do that their child might be Force-sensitive. Kegan, the planet is. Are you familiar with this world?"

He asked the question of Qui-Gon and Adi. Both Jedi Masters shook their heads. Obi-Wan was surprised. Between the two, they had traveled an extensive amount.

"Remote Kegan is," Yoda said. "A one-planet system orbiting one sun. It is an Outer Rim planet, cut off from the galaxy. Trade agreements, they do not have. Travel to other worlds, they do not do. Outsiders, they do not welcome. No one has landed on the planet in thirty years."

"That is very unusual," Qui-Gon observed.

Yoda blinked. He had lived long and seen much. There was not much that could surprise him.

"A good sign this request may be," he said. "Think we do that by taking this step Kegan means to open up relations with the Inner Core worlds. Welcomes this, the Galactic Senate does. Relations between worlds fosters peace. So two parts, your mission has. Open relations with Kegan we must. Determine the child's potential we must as well. A planet that isolates itself can be filled with suspicion and fear. Diplomatic you must be. Disruption you must not allow."

Yoda looked at Adi and Qui-Gon. Obi-Wan was confused. Was he sending the two Jedi Masters instead of a Master–Padawan team?

"Two teams we have decided to send," Yoda said.

"You mean all of us?" Obi-Wan blurted in dismay.

Yoda ignored his tone. "Cooperate you must to complete the mission."

Cooperate with Siri? Obi-Wan wanted to cry. He'd need more than the Force to accomplish that!

CHAPTER 2

Why two teams? Obi-Wan wondered as Adi piloted their craft toward the surface of Kegan. The mission to identify a Force-sensitive child was fairly routine.

Did it mean that the Council was still looking over his shoulder?

After he had left the Jedi for a short time, Obi-Wan had been put on probation. He had used the time to deepen his study of the Jedi path. The probation had been lifted, and he was once again an official Padawan learner. But did the Council still withhold their trust?

Over the past months, the process of repairing his ties with his Master had been satisfying for both of them. They had spent much time at the Temple, and also had roamed the galaxy together, observing other worlds and customs and helping when they could. Their bond had grown stronger.

Had the Council not seen this? Why were they paired with Adi and Siri?

"Landing in three minutes," Adi announced, breaking into his thoughts.

Obi-Wan stole a glance at Siri. Her face was passive as she gazed over the countryside below. She looked completely calm, but perhaps she hid nervousness well. Obi-Wan remembered how anxious he'd felt before his first mission. It was a new experience to leave the Temple and be thrust into the sometimes rough and violent galaxy. Obi-Wan leaned closer.

"Landing on a planet for the first time can be confusing," he told her. "There's usually so much to see that it's hard to focus. But in the first few minutes you can learn many things."

She didn't turn, but kept her eyes on the approaching landing platform. "I never lose my focus, Obi-Wan. Or my commitment."

The words felt like a slap. Obi-Wan leaned back again, his face flushed. Siri had been furious with him for leaving the Jedi path. She had accused him of undermining the commitment of all Padawans by his decision. She implied that her commitment to the Jedi was stronger than his.

It wasn't fair. He had taken one misstep. His Master and the Council had forgiven him. Why couldn't she?

The craft slowly lowered onto the landing platform. Obi-Wan saw a group waiting for them. Both the men and women wore tunics similar to the Jedis'.

Adi activated the ramp, and they disembarked. A man and a woman stepped forward immediately to greet them.

"Welcome, Jedi visitors," the woman said in a pleasant tone. She was of middle years, with a broad face and curly gray hair that framed her ruddy cheeks in a frothy cloud. "We are the Hospitality Guides, here to introduce you to our world and make sure you're comfortable. I am O-Rina and this is V-Haad."

Her companion smiled and bowed. He was tall and balding, with warm dark eyes.

The Jedi bowed in return, and Qui-Gon introduced them. "We were called here by two of your citizens."

The younger couple stepped forward. "I am V-Nen and this is my wife O-Melie," the man said. "We are the parents of O-Lana."

The woman's eyes studied them, then looked down. She seemed nervous, as did her husband. No doubt they were worried about the approaching examination of their child.

"The child is at their dwelling," V-Haad said. "We will transport you there. Please follow."

The Jedi followed the Guides and the parents to a battered-looking landspeeder. Obi-Wan had never seen such an old model in use. He wondered if it would be able to start.

The repulsorlift engine fired up with a worrisome clatter, but it ran perfectly. As they sped over the rugged ground, Obi-Wan looked around curiously. They were traveling along one central unpaved road that curved around a low wall. Inside the wall were domed structures. The landspeeders parked outside looked as ancient and battered as the one they were riding in.

"There is but one city on Kegan, and we are all its keepers," O-Rina shouted over the noise of the engine. "The rest of the planet is used for food and animal cultivation. There are large areas of open space. We are passing the Tech Circle right now. Kegan is divided into circles for each area of work. The Tech Circle leads into the Communication Circle, which leads to the Study Circle, which leads to the Garden Circle, and so on. They all ring the Gathering Circle, where we hold meetings. We are heading now to the Dwelling Circle."

A shadow passed over them, and Obi-Wan looked up. A skyhopper zoomed overhead, an old model he wasn't familiar with.

"Perhaps you are amazed that our transports are still running," V-Haad said to him with a chuckle. "Here on Kegan we do not destroy, we reuse. Our Tech Circle is expert at keeping old technology functional. We have no need for the newest models."

"Do you have currency here?" Adi Gallia asked in an interested way.

V-Haad shook his head. "We are a barter economy. Everything belongs to the General Good. We may give up great riches here, but we have no crime. I would rather live peacefully and safely than with worry on my shoulders."

"It seems a good philosophy," Qui-Gon agreed. "Do you have a system of government?"

"We have Benevolent Guides, V-Tan and O-Vieve," O-Rina said. "They were the first to devise a new way to live here on Kegan. They have an Advising Circle, but they guide rather than rule. We are all given a voice. Everything is adjusted for the General Good."

Obi-Wan had to admit that the system seemed to work on the surface. Perhaps because Kegan was a tiny planet with a small population, it managed to avoid the strife of other worlds. As they sped by, people lifted their heads from their tasks to wave and smile. They all seemed busy and happy.

Still, he noticed something strange. "I don't see any children," he said to the Guides.

"Children are precious here," O-Rina told him. "Education is very important. They are sent to school at an early age to learn and explore. Ah, here is the Dwelling Circle."

V-Haad piloted the craft through a break in the wall and guided it to a penned enclosure where a few battered landspeeders were parked. They walked toward one of the many domed buildings that curved around the core in a spiral. Each building was connected to the next.

V-Nen opened the door and stood aside to let them in. The small room was furnished simply but comfortably, with low benches piled with thick cushions.

Qui-Gon turned to V-Haad and O-Rina. "Thank you for bringing us here. We would like to examine the child alone with the parents."

"Oh, of course, we understand your procedures," V-Haad said.

"But we cannot follow them, so sorry to say this," O-Rina added. "O-Melie and V-Nen have asked us to stay. They are nervous with outsiders."

Qui-Gon looked at the parents kindly. "There is nothing to be nervous about. We will simply tell you if your child is Force-sensitive. If so, we will explain what that means and what can be done, should you wish it."

V-Nen and O-Melie exchanged glances. O-Melie swallowed. "We wish for the Hospitality Guides to stay."

V-Haad and O-Rina smiled. "You see? You must not think of us as outsiders in this house," O-Rina rushed to assure them. "Everyone on Kegan is part of the same family. This is true, O-Melie?"

"Yes," O-Melie said.

Suddenly, O-Rina and V-Haad's smiles seemed fixed to their faces, as though what was inside did not match their friendliness. A small trickle of warning snaked through Obi-Wan. He had learned to trust that feeling.

Something was wrong here. Things were not what they appeared to be. V-Haad and O-Rina had seemed to welcome them, but Obi-Wan had a feeling they were not happy the Jedi were here. Not at all.

CHAPTER 3

Qui-Gon didn't trust V-Haad and O-Rina from the start. Despite their wide smiles, they gave off a sense of unease that he could not attribute to being unused to strangers. And why were there Hospitality Guides when the planet allowed no visitors?

He nodded at them anyway, meeting their friendliness with his own. "Of course you may remain if V-Nen and O-Melie wish it," he said.

"There are exceptions to every rule," Adi said graciously. She, too, no doubt knew that it was better not to aggravate the situation by insisting.

"I'll get O-Lana," O-Melie said shortly. "A neighbor is watching her." She hurried from the room.

She returned in a moment with a small bundle in her arms. The child was close to a year old. She looked up at Qui-Gon with a bright, inquisitive gaze. He held out a finger. She grabbed it, then pulled it to her mouth and gnawed on it gently.

"Ah," Qui-Gon said. "I see." He studied her for some minutes, evaluating her reactions and expressions. Finally, he gave a short nod.

"You've reached your conclusion so soon?" O-Rina asked, her smile a little tight.

"Yes, I have," Qui-Gon answered. "She is definitely hungry."

O-Melie and V-Nen broke into relieved smiles.

"O-Yani can feed her," O-Rina suggested. "That way we can all talk."

"O-Yani is the child caregiver for this dwelling quad," V-Haad explained to the Jedi. "There is one for each quad in each dwelling circle so that parents may still work or have time for themselves. Our child caregivers are the wisest and best among us."

O-Melie took the baby from Qui-Gon's arms. She disappeared into the other room.

With only a quick glance at Adi, Qui-Gon knew that his fellow Jedi Master had also picked up what he had: O-Lana was Force-sensitive. But how deep the Force ran was something they needed more time to discover.

"Let us sit down," Adi suggested. "While the

child is feeding, we can explain more about why we have come so far to see her."

O-Melie and V-Nen sat down on a cushioned bench opposite from the Jedi. V-Haad sat on one side of them, O-Rina sat on the other. *As though they are guarding them,* Qui-Gon thought.

"If O-Lana is strong in the Force, her powers will become more apparent as she grows," Qui-Gon began. "These powers should be nurtured and directed. When they are not, the child can become confused and frightened."

V-Nen and O-Melie leaned closer, their eyes on the Jedi.

"No one is frightened on Kegan," O-Rina said firmly.

"The General Good is strong. O-Lana will be supported by us all," V-Haad added.

Adi spoke up. "The Temple on Coruscant is a place where a Force-sensitive child can learn not only how to control her gift, but how to let it guide her and connect her to all things."

V-Haad nodded, smiling. "Excellent! The Jedi Order sounds very wonderful indeed. We have Guides here that show us how to connect."

Adi stirred impatiently. Qui-Gon quickly stepped in.

"If O-Lana is a special child —"

"Ah, here I must interrupt you," O-Rina said, her smile beaming gracious friendship at Qui-Gon. "O-Lana is special, yes — but only as each Keganite is special. V-Tan and O-Vieve have taught us all that the Guide Within is powerful in each of us. No one is any better than another."

"We are not saying that O-Lana is better," Adi said. Qui-Gon could hear the impatience she was struggling to control. "We are saying that the Force will set her apart. The Jedi path will show her how to connect to the galaxy and to others."

V-Haad beamed. "Ah, now I see! A wise and just path, I'm sure. But O-Lana will have no need of this. Here on Kegan, each Guide Within unites and forms the General Good. It would be wrong to remove O-Lana from the circle of General Good, as the circle would diminish and O-Lana would be raised to believe she was special. This is against the counsel of the Guides." V-Haad and O-Rina nodded and smiled.

Slowly, V-Nen and O-Melie nodded, too.

Qui-Gon understood Adi's frustration. V-Nen and O-Melie seemed to be listening intently, but they were not given a chance to react. Instead, the Hospitality Guides were doing all the reacting and talking. This was precisely why the Jedi preferred the first interview to be with the parents only.

He knew that despite their interjections, V-Haad and O-Rina had not truly listened to a word the Jedi had said. They had asked no questions about the Jedi path, or about O-Lana's abilities. If it were up to them, this child would never leave Kegan.

Qui-Gon focused on V-Nen and O-Melie. "If O-Lana is strong in the Force, you need to fully understand what that means. She might be able to move objects, or see things before they happen. Such things can frighten a young child."

"Not on Kegan," O-Rina said cheerily. "Our Benevolent Guides themselves, O-Vieve and V-Tan, have visions. We have learned to trust them. Their visions of the future have guided the present, creating the General Good."

Qui-Gon exchanged a quick glance with Adi. They had to get the parents away from the Guides. That was clear. But they also had to be mindful of Yoda's directive. They could not bring disruption to this planet. They must respect the Kegans' way of doing things.

The Hospitality Guides suddenly stood. "That was an excellent meeting," V-Haad said. "I'm so glad to hear of the wonderful Jedi way."

"And we are sure you are tired from your

journey," O-Rina added. "We will show you to the quarters we have for you. There will be plenty of time for more discussion."

"Unless you must go," V-Haad said. "We know how important the Jedi are."

"We can stay as long as V-Nen and O-Melie want us to," Adi said firmly.

"I have a request," Qui-Gon said. "We would like to walk to our destination. We did have a long journey, it's true. We'd like to stretch our legs and see more of your beautiful planet."

The two Hospitality Guides exchanged glances at this unexpected request.

"Of course," O-Rina said, reluctance coloring her usual bright expression. "If you would like that . . ."

"We would," Qui-Gon said firmly. "And of course we would enjoy the company of V-Nen and O-Melie as well. It will give us a chance to get to know one other."

The Guides could not refuse. O-Melie and V-Nen went to ask their neighbor O-Yani if she could continue watching O-Lana.

"The baby is sleeping now," O-Melie said quietly as she slipped back inside. "We would be happy to walk with you."

The Guides and O-Melie and V-Nen went out. Under the cover of adjusting his cloak, Qui-Gon turned back to Obi-Wan and Siri.

"Leave us and wander off when you can," he said in a low tone. "Do it without being seen. The Guides will come after you. Avoid them. You can use the time to gather information about Kegan. Do not cause disruption or upset. Remember, observation without interference. Do not reveal that you are Jedi."

Obi-Wan and Siri nodded, their expressions alert.

Qui-Gon saw Adi's worried look. He thought he understood. They would cause a disruption. A minimal disruption, and worth the risk, in his opinion. But Adi might not think so. He was not used to having to ask another Jedi Master to approve a course of action. He waited, his eyes on her, to see if she would object.

As he waited, Qui-Gon wondered again why Yoda had sent two teams to this planet. Had Adi been sent in order to monitor his tendency to follow his instincts and bend the rules? Was she meant to oversee how he and Obi-Wan worked together?

And if she did not approve of his suggestion, what would he do?

But Adi nodded. "This had better work," she murmured as she stepped out into the bright sunlight.

CHAPTER 4

"Tell me, V-Haad and O-Rina," Qui-Gon said as they walked through the streets of Kegan. "I see that you have solved many problems that other worlds have not. Why don't Keganites travel to other worlds and share knowledge with them?"

"We have no need to," V-Haad said. "We have what we need for a good life here. And travel can be dangerous. The galaxy is a violent place. If we traveled it would encourage others to travel here. That could bring danger to Kegan. You can't deny that there is violence throughout the galaxy."

"No, I cannot," Qui-Gon agreed. "But there is also trade and an exchange of knowledge."

O-Rina and V-Haad merely smiled and shook their heads.

"We have everything we need," V-Haad repeated. "Importing trade or knowledge is un-necessary and harmful to the General Good."

"Why would advances in knowledge be harmful?" Obi-Wan asked, curious.

Qui-Gon saw a red flush mount on V-Haad's neck, even while his smile stayed fixed on his face.

"Kegan is a beautiful planet," Adi remarked in an obvious attempt to change the subject.

Quickly, O-Rina switched the topic to the lovely spaces of Kegan, pointing out native species as they passed the Garden Circle with its blooming flowers.

Qui-Gon remained silent. There was something else bothering him about Kegan — something besides the determined smiles on the faces of the Hospitality Guides. Suddenly he realized he had not heard laughter since he'd landed on the planet. He had not seen any public sculptures or fountains or works of art. He had not heard music. On such a peaceful planet it was unusual. Perhaps it was the lack of joy — despite the smiles — that was disturbing him.

"Here is our marketplace," O-Rina said proudly, sweeping an arm to show them the circular area crowded with stalls. "No one needs currency to buy. Everyone barters with their own surplus. No one goes hungry."

It was the oddest marketplace Qui-Gon had ever seen. Although they had just passed fruit orchards in the Garden Circle and had seen trees with boughs bent with ripe fruit, there was not a fresh fruit or vegetable to be seen. Strips of dried fruit and vegetables hung from hooks, and large bins contained grains. There were cobblers for boots and tailors who sold tunics and work gear. Shoppers went about their business with smiles and nods. They did not linger with pleasure at a display or stop to be tempted by a treat. There was plenty to see in the market, but nothing enticing to buy.

"Very . . . useful," Siri said politely.

A cart headed for them, loaded with bolts of rough linen. Qui-Gon stepped quickly to his right, seeming to get out of the way. He stepped into the path of a stall keeper who was placing tools on a rack for display. The rack tilted, and the tools spilled into the path.

Quickly, Qui-Gon bent down to help the stall keeper pick up the tools. When he stood, Obi-Wan and Siri were gone.

O-Rina turned. "You see, new goods arrive constantly. Here on Kegan, we . . ." Her voice trailed off. Her eyes raked over the surrounding area. "But what has happened to your young Jedi?"

V-Haad swiveled, trying to take in the crowd. "Did they stop behind us?"

"I'm not sure," Qui-Gon said, pretending to search the crowd. "Perhaps they saw something that interested them."

"They haven't seen any of your technology," Adi offered. "Perhaps they were interested in those old transmitters we saw."

"Yes, curiosity. Very commendable, but we should find them," O-Rina babbled. "So easy to get lost on Kegan."

"Not a good idea to get lost," V-Haad confirmed. "The Circles can be confusing, like a maze."

O-Rina and V-Haad looked at V-Nen and O-Melie.

"If you will wait here with the Jedi . . ." O-Rina said.

"And show them the market . . ." V-Haad added.

"But do not go far," O-Rina said. "Or else we would be unable to find you. That would distress us."

She is warning them, Qui-Gon thought.

"We will wait here," V-Nen said quietly. Qui-Gon saw him reach for O-Melie's hand.

The Hospitality Guides rushed off. Qui-Gon turned to V-Nen and O-Melie. A skyhopper engine buzzed overhead, and he spoke underneath its noise. "We are grateful for this opportunity to talk to you alone."

"We have nothing more to say." O-Melie's voice was flat. "We made a mistake in contacting you. You should go."

Qui-Gon exchanged a puzzled glance with Adi. He had imagined that O-Melie and V-Nen were bursting with questions behind their silence.

V-Nen put a hand on his wife's arm. Qui-Gon noted that she was trembling. What was going on? He felt frustration well in him. How could he and Adi get through to the parents? They were obviously afraid.

"O-Lana could be awake now," he said. "Why don't we go to see her again? You should know if O-Lana is indeed strong in the Force, even if you do not make a decision now. You can think about it."

"Let us return and examine the child," Adi Gallia added softly. "We will tell you what we think, and then we will go."

V-Nen and O-Melie hesitated. Qui-Gon could see that they wanted to agree.

"We will take complete responsibility with the Hospitality Guides," Qui-Gon added.

"All right," V-Nen said reluctantly.

V-Nen led them in a snaking path through the marketplace. They came out on a different road than the one they had taken before. He led them down backstreets, this time ending up in the back of their dwelling.

They followed the parents inside. As they entered their dwelling, an elder woman emerged. She had close-cropped russet hair threaded with silver and small dark eyes that darted nervously, like a bird's.

"You've returned," she said.

"Where is Lana, O-Yani?" O-Melie asked. "Is she sleeping?"

"She is not here," the older woman replied. "They came. They took her away."

CHAPTER 5

Obi-Wan and Siri did not run, or even appear to hurry. They had been taught how to move through a crowd without being seen. By the time the person turned to look at them, Siri and Obi-Wan had already melted farther into the crowd.

They left the marketplace behind, sure that O-Rina and V-Haad would comb it thoroughly.

"Let's head for the Garden Circle," Obi-Wan suggested. "It will be easier to hide there."

Siri nodded. They hurried toward the circle and ran down a path that wound through rows of leafy trees. Spotting a forested area ahead, they headed for it. They struggled through tall overgrown shrubs studded with brambles that choked the narrow trail. Finally, they stopped in a clearing to catch their breath.

Siri pulled a bramble out of her hair. "I don't

know why we had to leave at all," she grumbled. "Just when things were getting interesting, Qui-Gon comes up with a plan to get rid of us. How am I going to learn if I never get to watch two Jedi Masters in action?"

"The mission is what drives us," Obi-Wan said.

Siri tore another bramble from her blond hair. "You don't have to repeat Jedi wisdom to me, Obi-Wan. I took the same classes you did."

Suddenly, she sighed and flopped back onto the soft grass. "I'm just disappointed. I wanted to see how Qui-Gon and Adi would handle this. Something is very strange on this planet. Those Hospitality Guides gave me the shivers. Who knew a smile could be so eerie?"

"That's why Qui-Gon wanted to see the parents alone," Obi-Wan told her.

Siri gave him a sidelong look that seemed like pure disgust. "You don't have to explain the plan to me. I was there."

She jumped up before he could react. She was always doing that, Obi-Wan thought. She never gave him a chance to apologize or explain. Not that he wanted to.

"Come on," she said. "We shouldn't stay in one place for too long."

"I know that," Obi-Wan said, moving ahead.

Siri picked up her pace, and they hurried through the overgrown paths. Neither would let the other lead.

This is ridiculous, Obi-Wan thought. *Haven't I learned anything in all my years at the Temple? I shouldn't be competing with Siri.*

But he couldn't fall back and let her lead, either.

"Maybe we should find the Tech Circle," Obi-Wan suggested. "If we're supposed to investigate how the society really works here on Kegan, it seems like a good place to start."

"That's the first place they'd look for us," Siri scoffed.

They emerged from the bushy overgrowth and found themselves alongside a field of tall grass. A dirt path ran along the edge of the field, and they turned down it.

"Do you have a better suggestion?" Obi-Wan asked.

"I think we should mingle with the people," Siri said. "It's a human population, so we'll mix in. And we wear similar clothes, too. We might be able to pick up lots of information just by talking to people."

Before Obi-Wan could reply, the noise of an engine split the air. A landspeeder was approaching. It was too late to retreat into the shrubbery.

"Let's try to bluff," he murmured to Siri.

The landspeeder drew up alongside them. A burly middle-aged man dressed in a chroma-sheath tunic smiled at them in a friendly way.

"What are you two doing out here?"

"Just out walking," Obi-Wan said.

"No school today?" the man asked in a pleasant tone.

Here was a trap. Obi-Wan didn't want to say they were visitors. That would surely send O-Rina and V-Haad on their trail.

"We have permission to be out," Siri said. "Our parents need help at home. Speaking of which, we'd better head there."

"Suit yourself." The man waved them on.

They began to walk past him. But something was wrong. The Force surged, warning Obi-Wan a moment before an electro-jabber swiped at his knees, then his shoulder. They were both glancing blows, enough to send Obi-Wan crashing to the ground. A split second later, Siri crashed next to him. Her breath left her in a hiss. She had never felt an electro-jabber before.

The man picked them up and dumped them like cargo on the rear floor of the landspeeder. Then they roared off.

CHAPTER 6

"O-Lana is gone?" O-Melie's face went dead white. She stumbled backward, and V-Nen steadied her. She pressed a hand to her mouth. "How could you have let her go?"

"I had to," O-Yani replied, her eyes darting from O-Melie to V-Nen. "They said she was due for her routine med check. There is no reason for concern. She will come back. She will not disappear."

V-Nen shot a glance at O-Melie. *A warning glance,* Qui-Gon thought. He saw O-Melie swallow. The look on her face was transformed. Her constricted facial muscles smoothed out. Her lips tilted upward in a strained smile.

"Of course," she said. "I understand."

They heard the sound of running footsteps, and the Hospitality Guides hurried toward them.

"Ah, we found you!" O-Rina said.

V-Haad's smile did not falter. "We thought you were to wait in the market."

"We must have misunderstood," Qui-Gon said. "We asked if we could return here. So sorry if we caused you upset."

"O-Lana has been taken," O-Melie said, struggling to keep a pleasant expression on her face. "O-Yani says the Med Circle Guides came for her. But she just had her routine med exam. Perhaps there is some mistake."

"We shall check on it," O-Rina assured her. "Do not be concerned. A child can't be too healthy!"

V-Nen looked as ashen as his wife, but his face was frozen into the same pleasant mask. "Parental notification before a med check always takes place. Strange that O-Lana was taken without it."

"Slips can occur, even on Kegan," V-Haad said in a jovial tone. "But that doesn't excuse them," he added quickly.

"Even a moment of worry about a child can be an eternity," O-Rina said sympathetically. "V-Haad and I will be happy to intercede for you. We'll go right to V-Tan and O-Vieve if we have to."

"We are grateful," V-Nen said through tight lips.

O-Rina turned to the Jedi. "Of course, all this

will take time. We know the Jedi are far too crucial to the galaxy to linger. We will completely understand if you must return to your more important tasks."

"Unfortunately we did not find your young aides," V-Haad said pleasantly. "Perhaps you have communication devices that can summon them."

"Thank you for your concern," Qui-Gon answered smoothly. "But I'm afraid you overestimate our demand in the galaxy. We can certainly remain here until the child is found. As for our aides, I'm afraid we're at a loss."

Adi picked up on his strategy. "We have tried to contact them on our comlinks," she said. "They are not responding. Perhaps they lost them, or our technology does not work on your planet. We will have to search for them."

"We are sorry if this causes trouble for you," Qui-Gon added. "We would like permission to travel among your people. You know how the young can be. They are most likely exploring and have forgotten the time."

The Hospitality Guides were trapped. They could not refuse such a sensible request. But they looked uncertain.

"Kegan is a peaceful planet," V-Haad said haltingly. "Yet our people are unused to foreigners. They could feel fear, which could make them act in unaccustomed ways. We wouldn't want you to run into trouble of any kind . . ."

"Jedi are used to walking among strangers," Adi said, inclining her head. "We are not worried."

"We will be in touch," Qui-Gon said, bowing to the Guides.

The Guides turned away. O-Melie stayed still as a block of stone, but her burning eyes beseeched the Jedi. *Find her!*

Then the Hospitality Guides turned back again, and her bland smile returned.

"The mother is frightened," Adi said.

"The father as well," Qui-Gon said. "He hides it slightly better."

Adi sighed. They had paused by the Gardening Circle before going on. "I am afraid that with every step we take, we violate the Council's wishes. We are interfering. We could make enemies here."

"A child is missing," Qui-Gon said. "Never mind that she is Force-sensitive. Her parents are obviously terrified. The situation has changed. And it is because of our presence. If we had not come, the child would be safe."

Adi nodded reluctantly. "The child could be

where the Guides say she is. They want to keep us away from her. That doesn't mean they'll harm her. We can't take bold action without ascertaining if the child is in danger."

Qui-Gon knew the child wasn't safe — why else would the parents be so afraid? But he held his tongue. He and Adi Gallia needed to work as a team.

Adi went on thoughtfully. "Our mission is also to demonstrate to Kegan the benefits of joining the galactic alliance. We are promoting peace. All I am saying is that we must tread carefully."

"We are telling each other things we already know," Qui-Gon said restlessly. "Let's raise Obi-Wan and Siri on their comlinks."

He activated his comlink, but Obi-Wan did not answer. Adi did the same with hers, but there was no answer from Siri, either.

"Perhaps they're in a situation where it is better not to answer," Adi suggested. "We told them to mingle with the native population and not advertise that they were Jedi."

"True," Qui-Gon agreed. "Let's try again later. In the meantime, searching for them will give us a good cover to look for O-Lana. Let's head for the Med Circle."

They roamed through the various clinics,

looking into nurseries and care centers. No one stopped them. In their rough tunics with their lightsabers hidden, they could pass for native Keganites.

"If we could access their records . . ." Qui-Gon murmured to Adi.

"That would involve violating their security," she said with a shake of her head. "A serious breach of conduct."

"But it's the only way," Qui-Gon argued. "Obviously they've hidden the child."

"We should keep searching," Adi said firmly.

Qui-Gon had a hard time suppressing his frustration. Cooperation among Jedi was a given. It was how they were raised to interact. But what happened when they disagreed?

"For a little longer," he said.

She arched an eyebrow at him. Tall and forbidding, with dark golden skin and blue facial markings, Adi Gallia was known to subdue a boisterous group of young students with just a glance. Qui-Gon was not as easily intimidated.

"There you are!" They heard O-Rina's chirping tone behind them. "Have you found your young aides? Strange that you are looking in the Med Circle."

"Young Jedi are interested in all facets of society," Adi answered, composed.

"And how is the search for O-Lana?" Qui-Gon asked. "Strange that three people have disappeared in one morning."

"We have put another team on the problem," V-Haad said quickly. "O-Vieve and V-Tan thought it best."

"Perhaps we should speak with your Benevolent Guides," Qui-Gon said. "We would like permission to search the records of Kegan."

V-Haad was already shaking his head. "We would do anything for the Jedi. But appointments with V-Tan and O-Vieve must be requested weeks in advance. They are very busy."

"But you said they just saw you," Adi pointed out.

"This is true," O-Rina said, her ruddy cheeks deepening in color. "We are high-level Guides, you see."

"I think you will find that they will see us," Qui-Gon said firmly. "Shall we go together, or will you point the way?"

His tone told them he would not take no for an answer. O-Rina and V-Haad nodded reluctantly. "Of course, we are at the Jedi's service . . ."

Qui-Gon echoed the blank smile of the Guides. "Then lead on."

CHAPTER 7

"I still can't feel my legs," Siri whispered. Obi-Wan could hear the fear in her voice.

"It will wear off," he assured her. "But it will take a few hours."

They had been traveling for some time. The city had been left behind. From his position on the floor of the speeder, Obi-Wan could see a glimpse of sky. He had seen no other speeders around them for kilometers now, just the top branches of the trees, dancing in a brisk breeze. The temperature was dropping; perhaps they were heading to a higher altitude.

At last the engines thrummed to a lower speed and they stopped. The door next to Obi-Wan opened and he was dragged out roughly. His legs were too unsteady to hold him and he was dumped on the ground. Siri was dumped next to him.

"I thought children were revered on Kegan," Obi-Wan said, his cheek in the dirt.

A boot was suddenly placed on his head. His face was pushed farther into the dirt. "No back talk. You know very well that truancy is a criminal act on Kegan. You're old enough to be punished for it."

"But we're not Keganites!" Siri protested.

"I've heard all the excuses. Shut your mouth."

"We're from another world. We're visitors," Siri insisted furiously. "Take your boot off my friend's head."

The boot was removed from Obi-Wan's head and landed on Siri's shoulder. "Sure," the man said.

Enough, Obi-Wan thought. He struggled to rise, but the electro-jabber had done its work. He knew he wouldn't regain full use of his arms and legs for several more hours. It would be impossible to use his lightsaber effectively until then. Besides, he'd been instructed not to show Keganites that he was a Jedi. Obi-Wan tried to roll closer to Siri but couldn't move. He watched helplessly as the boot increased pressure on Siri's shoulder, driving her face into the dirt.

"What did I say about back talk?" the man asked again.

Siri gritted her teeth. Her vivid blue eyes

blazed. She spat out the dirt in her mouth. Still, she didn't answer.

"V-Tarz!" A voice boomed from behind them. Instantly, V-Tarz took his boot off Siri's shoulder.

Obi-Wan saw another man approach, wearing the same navy chromasheath tunic as V-Tarz.

"Why are these students on the ground?" the second man demanded.

"Resisting capture," V-Tarz responded.

"No need to use physical force," the other man said. "We've discussed this before. The Learning works with love, not fear. Take them to class."

Obi-Wan was hauled to his feet. He locked his knees so that he would not fall. Siri did the same.

"But we're not Keganites," Obi-Wan protested to the second guard, who seemed more friendly. "We're visitors."

The second guard's dark gaze flicked over Obi-Wan and Siri. "No one visits Kegan. Three marks for lying." He turned away. "Take them to class."

V-Tarz nudged them with the handle end of his electro-jabber. "You heard V-Brose. Get moving."

"Let's make a break for it," Siri murmured to Obi-Wan as they stumbled across the yard, their muscles like pudding.

"Are you kidding? We wouldn't last five meters," Obi-Wan whispered through his teeth. "We have to wait until the effect of the electro-jabber wears off. We'll figure out where we are and contact Qui-Gon and Adi Gallia."

"Just let me at V-Tarz before we get out of here," Siri muttered.

"That does not sound like a Jedi," Obi-Wan said disapprovingly. "V-Tarz is not our enemy, merely an obstacle to our mission."

"That *obstacle* just ground the faces of two helpless young people into the dirt," Siri responded. "Just what do you require in an enemy, Obi-Wan?"

Their conversation stopped abruptly as V-Tarz pushed them against a wall. Rough hands reached under Obi-Wan's travel cloak. V-Tarz brought out Obi-Wan's lightsaber and examined it.

"What is this?"

Obi-Wan tensed. He could not lose his lightsaber without a fight, no matter how weak he was.

"It's just a hand-warming device," Siri said.

V-Tarz shoved it back in Obi-Wan's belt. "Then I don't need it. What's this . . . ?"

He'd found Obi-Wan's comlink. He pulled it out of its pouch, then grabbed Siri's.

"You won't be needing these," V-Tarz said,

holding them up. "They look new," he said, examining them. "Your parents must work in the Comm Circle in order to have comlinks like these." He stuck them in his pocket, a delighted smile on his face. Obi-Wan was afraid he'd take their electrobinoculars next.

"For the last time, slab-brain, we're not Keganites," Siri snapped.

V-Tarz raised the electro-jabber. Obi-Wan tensed. Another blow could put Siri out of commission for a very long time.

A carved bust of a serene-looking woman sat on a high shelf over them. Obi-Wan called on the Force. The bust rocketed to the edge of the shelf and flew off. It missed V-Tarz by millimeters and crashed to the floor, sending chips of marble everywhere. V-Tarz stared down at it in disbelief.

A door near them opened. A Keganite woman stuck her head in. Her hair was pulled back behind her ears in a severe style, and she wore a plain brown tunic over black trousers.

"V-Tarz! What's going on? I'm trying to conduct a class." Her gaze traveled over the broken bust. "You smashed O-Vieve!"

"It fell, O-Bin," V-Tarz said. "An unfortunate accident. But here are two students for you. Keep your excellent eye on them — they're troublemakers."

O-Bin cast a cool gaze over Siri and Obi-Wan. Then she smiled. Obi-Wan felt a chill move through him. The smile was eerily similar to O-Rina's and V-Haad's.

"There are no troublemakers in The Learning," O-Bin said. "Come."

Glad to get away from V-Tarz, Obi-Wan and Siri followed the teacher through the durasteel door into the classroom. The door clanged shut behind them and an automatic lock snapped shut.

Students dressed in gray tunics sat on long benches that ran the width of the room, row after row. Small data screens rose from the floor in front of each of them at eye-level. The students sat erect, hands at their sides. Only their eyes moved as they examined Obi-Wan and Siri.

"I'm afraid there's been a mistake," Siri said to O-Bin. "We aren't Keganites. We're . . ."

Obi-Wan heard a few titters from the class. A slight, sandy-haired boy with hair that brushed his shoulders gave him a sympathetic look, then quickly looked down at his data screen. O-Bin swiveled and fixed her smiling gaze on row after row. The room went still.

"Sit," she told Siri and Obi-Wan.

"But we are not —" Obi-Wan began.

"Sit." The smile didn't waver. "Put on the

robes for The Learning." She handed them two gray tunics.

Obi-Wan and Siri exchanged glances. Should they continue to resist, or give in for now? Mindful of Qui-Gon's orders, Obi-Wan slipped into the tunic. Siri did the same.

The same slender boy moved over to make room for them. Obi-Wan and Siri sat. Immediately two data screens rose in front of them.

The teacher looked at them, her fingers poised over her datapad. "Names, please."

"Obi-Wan Kenobi," Obi-Wan said. "Of Coruscant."

"Three marks for lying," O-Bin said, smiling. "One mark for not giving your full name."

"That is my full name!" Obi-Wan protested.

"Three more marks for lying," O-Bin said. "I see you already have three. That makes . . . ten marks. Class?"

"Marks reveal the Inner Guide's confusion," the class chanted in unison.

"V-Obi is confused," the teacher said, nodding. "His Inner Guide is cloudy. It is up to all of you to bring him to his contribution to the General Good."

The class nodded solemnly.

"Have we landed on Weird World?" Siri whispered to Obi-Wan.

"Two marks for talking, and what is your name?" The teacher turned to Siri.

"Siri —"

"One mark for not giving your full name, O-Siri," the teacher said. "We each have a letter before our names that we share with others. This demonstrates our commitment to the General Good. Class?"

"We are all unique, yet none is better than another. Such is the General Good," the class chanted.

"This is generally crazy," Siri muttered.

"Three marks for talking after being warned, O-Siri," O-Bin said. "Let us return to the lesson."

Obi-Wan's data screen flashed blue. Letters began to crawl across the screen:

TRAVEL TO THE INNER CORE IS DANGEROUS. THE FIRST OBSTACLE IS THE DELACRIX SYSTEM.

Obi-Wan frowned. He knew the Delacrix System. They'd passed it on the way to Kegan. Qui-Gon had said it was a thriving system of planets orbiting around three suns. All the worlds traded together in harmony. They had all recently joined the Galactic Senate.

"Who can tell me why the Delacrix System is dangerous?" the teacher asked. "O-Iris?"

"The Delacrix System is dangerous because

it is controlled by pirates," a small, red-haired girl said in an almost-whisper. "Its third sun is in perpetual nova, so it can melt the engines of passing craft. The pirates divert passing traffic into the outer edges of the exploding sun to force a landing."

Obi-Wan stared at the small girl in amazement. Everything she'd said was untrue.

Observation without interference, Qui-Gon had said. If he kept his mouth closed, he could learn.

Just as Obi-Wan resolved to stay silent no matter what, Siri spoke up.

"But that's not true!" she protested.

"I did not call on you, O-Siri," O-Bin said severely. "If you wish to ask a question, touch your data screen."

Siri touched her data screen.

O-Bin's lips were tight as she smiled and turned back to her. "Yes, O-Siri?"

"The Delacrix System is not overrun by pirates," Siri said.

"That is not a question," O-Bin said. Her cheeks flushed red. "Two marks."

"And its sun is not in perpetual nova," Siri added. "It's a peaceful system with a thriving trade."

"Three marks." O-Bin's smile was forced. "That makes eleven marks all together. You have caught up to your stubborn companion."

"Come on, Obi-Wan," Siri muttered without moving her lips. "Give me a hand here."

Obi-Wan sighed. He touched his data screen. "Question, V-Obi?"

"Delacrix is a safe, peaceful system," Obi-Wan said. "Travel is not dangerous. Caution is required, but —"

"Four marks for disobedience!" O-Bin's voice screeched. She cleared her throat and smiled. "You are not contributing to the General Good. Now we turn to the next outlying system. Please consult your screens."

The words scrolled across Obi-Wan's screen.

THE PLANET STIEG PRESENTS MORE HAZZARDS.

"Can anyone say why?" O-Bin asked, facing the class. "V-Davi?"

The slender, sandy-haired boy spoke up. "Stieg has no organized government or ruling system. Tribes are locked in constant warfare."

Siri stood up on legs that still trembled from the effects of the electro-jabber. "Hold on. The Stieg-Fan are peaceful and fun-loving. And Stieg has a perfectly fine system of government!"

O-Bin's face grew flushed. "Thank you for your contribution, O-Siri, but it is a *lie.*"

"I don't lie!"

Obi-Wan wanted to tug on Siri's tunic to make her sit down. But he couldn't undo what she'd already said. He'd have to back her up.

"Siri is right. Stieg is peaceful," Obi-Wan said.

O-Bin seemed about to explode. She squeezed her hands together. Then, she smiled.

"You two make it difficult to keep up with how many punishment marks you have," she said in a tone that hit each word like a sharp rap against a tuneless bell. "I'm afraid greater punishment is called for. You will both clean up the food service area for the entire school after the evening meal."

The sandy-haired student called V-Davi looked at them sympathetically.

"Think again," Siri shot back. "I don't have to follow your rules. I'm not under your authority!"

"If you choose to refuse your punishment and hurt the General Good," O-Bin continued, "not one student will eat today."

Fifty pairs of angry eyes turned and stared at Obi-Wan and Siri.

"Now, do you still refuse?" O-Bin asked.

Under cover of his tunic, Obi-Wan nudged Siri to silence. He would not be responsible for depriving the students of food. When they didn't respond, O-Bin turned away, a smug smile of satisfaction on her face.

"Great," Siri whispered. "Not only are we trapped, we're trapped with dirty dishes."

O-Bin didn't turn. "Four punishment marks, O-Siri," she said sweetly.

CHAPTER 8

Qui-Gon and Adi stood in the middle of the Gathering Circle. Around them rose an open-air coliseum with stone slabs serving as benches.

"All Keganites participate in the governing of Kegan," V-Haad said proudly. "V-Tan and O-Vieve bring problems to the people. They do not supply solutions, merely proposals. Every citizen gets a vote."

A low, circular building was built next to the coliseum. In one of the few examples of finery on Kegan, its dome was painted gold.

"Here is the Central Dwelling, where our Benevolent Guides reside," O-Rina said. "We will request an audience for you."

O-Rina and V-Haad brought them to a small room with whitewashed walls that contained benches for seating. "They will be with you shortly," O-Rina said. "We'll await you at the front entrance."

In moments the door opened and two elder Keganites in soft white robes appeared. The woman's silver hair was braided and hung down her back. The man's was silver as well. Their beaming smiles seemed more sincere than those of the Hospitality Guides.

"Welcome, Qui-Gon Jinn and Adi Gallia," the woman said. "I am O-Vieve, and this is V-Tan. It is our honor to greet you."

The two Jedi bowed.

"We hope that you will be able to assist us," Qui-Gon said. "We arrived with our Padawans, Siri and Obi-Wan. They wandered off and we have been unable to find them."

V-Tan folded his hands. "The Hospitality Guides have informed us of this. We are concerned."

"We have decided to launch a search," O-Vieve said. "We will inform our citizens that the children are missing. We should have results very soon."

"We should like to join in the search," Qui-Gon said.

O-Vieve nodded at him sympathetically. "I feel your concern, yet you do not know our world. We can search quicker and more efficiently. V-Tan and I would be grateful if you would accept our hospitality during this short time. We have guest quarters prepared here in the Central Dwelling. I am certain you need food and rest. We will bring your Padawans to you."

Qui-Gon was about to protest, but Adi nodded. "Thank you," she said.

V-Tan and O-Vieve murmured that it was no trouble at all, and they were happy to be able to meet the gracious and kind Jedi. The Hospitality Guides would be waiting in the front reception hallway to show them the way to their rooms.

Qui-Gon and Adi strode into the hallway. As soon as they were out of earshot, Qui-Gon murmured, "We can't rely on them to search."

"Of course not," Adi agreed. "But if we had continued to protest, it wouldn't have done any good. They wouldn't have given in. They are not afraid of us the way O-Rina and V-Haad are."

"Afraid of us?" Qui-Gon asked, startled. "Nervous, perhaps. But why would they be afraid of us?"

"That is something I do not know," Adi said. "Yet."

Qui-Gon paused. The reception area was just ahead, and he did not want the Hospitality Guides to see them. "We need to go back to the beginning. We need to talk to V-Nen and O-Melie. Perhaps Obi-Wan and Siri's failure to come back is linked to O-Lana's disappearance."

Adi nodded. "How can we avoid O-Rina and V-Haad?"

"This way," Qui-Gon said, turning and heading back down the hallway. He turned to the left, then the right.

"How do you know where to go?" Adi asked.

Qui-Gon smiled. "While I was at the Temple, I took sensory lessons from Jedi Master Tahl. When she was blinded, she learned to improve her other senses. I'm following my sense of smell."

Adi concentrated. "Food. Something is cooking."

"And where there is food, there is waste. Where there is waste, there is usually an exit," Qui-Gon explained.

"And I always look for a window," Adi said, hurrying beside him.

The kitchen was empty except for a cook who was grinding a vegetable into a paste, his back to the door. Qui-Gon and Adi Gallia moved swiftly and silently past him and slipped out the door into a small area with waste bins. They skirted them and headed back in the direction they had come.

The distance wasn't far, and soon they stood

at V-Nen and O-Melie's door. Qui-Gon knocked softly.

V-Nen opened it. The hopeful expression on his face faded when he saw the Jedi.

"I thought there was word of Lana," he said.

"You must trust us," Adi told him. "We can help you protect your daughter."

O-Melie joined her husband at the door.

"We have nothing more to say," V-Nen said. "I must head for work at the Communications Circle now."

"We are late and must be going," O-Melie said. "Please do not follow us."

O-Melie's words were cool, but her eyes pleaded with them. What was she asking?

Before they could react, she shut the door in their faces.

Adi looked at Qui-Gon. The glance they exchanged was full of meaning. They did not speak for a moment as a skyhopper buzzed overhead.

"I suppose we should head back," Adi said.

"Yes," Qui-Gon agreed. "We can do no good here."

They turned and left the Dwelling Circle. But hope rose in Qui-Gon's heart. At last he was beginning to understand.

CHAPTER 9

Siri heaved another tub of dirty dishes into the sink. Sudsy water slopped on the floor.

"What slab-brain decided that turbo dish-cleaners were bad for the General Good?" she asked, picking up a cleaning rag.

"Menial labor attentively completed adds to the General Good," Obi-Wan said.

She shot him a sidelong look. "You sound like one of them."

"It's starting to sink in." Obi-Wan dried the last dish from the enormous rack and placed it on a pile.

Siri gazed out at the narrow band of windows that ran along the top of the wall. All the windows at the Learning Circle were set high in the walls. They allowed light in, but restricted a view of outside. They had been told that afternoon that contemplation of the outdoors was a waste of time they should be devoting to The Learning.

"It's getting dark," Siri said. "I say we break out tonight. We still have our lightsabers."

"I think we should wait," Obi-Wan said.

"For what?" Siri asked, rinsing off a plate. "The breakfast dishes?"

Obi-Wan spoke calmly. "For several things. One, we don't know what kind of security the Learning Circle has. We should discover that before we try. Remember that Qui-Gon and Adi told us not to cause disruption."

"But that was before we were captured," Siri argued.

"I know," Obi-Wan said. "No doubt they are worried by now. But that's still not a reason to try a risky escape. If we plan it, we might be able to avoid a fight."

Siri gazed at him in disbelief. "Is that all you care about? Avoiding a fight?"

Obi-Wan struggled to hold on to his temper. "I've learned on missions with Qui-Gon that it is always best to avoid a fight if you can. You should have learned that at the Temple."

Siri flushed pink. She knew that Obi-Wan was right. A Jedi always sought to avoid a conflict. *Infinitely more ways there are to reach a goal,* Yoda had said many times. *Try them all you should.*

"You seem to forget that we're Jedi," she said. "If we just reveal that we are, they'd let us go. They'd know that we aren't Keganites then."

"But we don't *know* that they'd let us go," Obi-Wan countered. "It's an option, but I still think we should wait. Qui-Gon told us not to reveal that we are Jedi. And Yoda told us to avoid disruption at all costs. Until we absolutely have to, I say we stay undercover. What if we're really being held because we *are* Jedi? Or what if we get Qui-Gon and Adi Gallia in trouble by proving that we're Jedi? We don't know what our Masters are up to right now." Obi-Wan shook his head. "There are too many questions. Unless we can find a way to leave quietly, we should remain for the time being. Think of it this way — we can learn about Kegan society here. This is like an indoctrination camp."

"Are you always so cautious?" Siri asked him.

"I wasn't always," Obi-Wan answered. "But now I am."

He met her gaze steadily. She knew what he was referring to. He had acted impulsively once, and almost lost his way. Now he knew: It was always tempting to act. It was often wiser to wait.

Frustrated, Siri threw the cleaning rag into the sink. It slapped against the water and sent another shower of suds onto the floor. Obi-Wan sighed. After the dish cleaning, there would be plenty of mopping to do, too.

"So we have to stay and listen to lies while we clean up after the whole school?" Siri asked, disgusted.

"We wouldn't have been forced to clean up if you didn't keep correcting O-Bin," Obi-Wan observed mildly.

"And let that teacher fill the students' minds with lies?" Siri asked in disbelief. "How can we do that, Obi-Wan? You know that everything they teach here is wrong."

"What you said didn't make a difference," Obi-Wan argued. "No one believed us, and we got stuck with cleaning detail."

"So this is all my fault," Siri said.

"It's not up to me to assign blame," Obi-Wan said testily. "But if you insist, yes!"

"You're the one who didn't want to break out when we could!" Siri exploded. "We should have made a run for it."

Obi-Wan opened his mouth to refute her, but a hesitant voice came from behind him.

"That wouldn't have been a good idea."

They turned. V-Davi, the slight boy from class, stood in the doorway. His hands were stuffed in the pockets of his tunic.

"The Security Guides have great power here," he said. "It's not wise to oppose them. And besides, it's against the General Good."

"Thanks for the tip," Obi-Wan said.

Siri picked up a mop and began to clean up the water and suds she'd spilled. "Why are you here, V-Davi?" she asked in a kindly way. "You don't have punishment marks too, do you?"

"No. I have food preparation duty tomorrow. I thought I would get a head start tonight." V-Davi headed for a bin of vegetables. He started up a grinding machine and began to toss them in.

"You mean they actually prepare the stuff they serve?" Siri grumbled. "I thought they just scooped it out of the trash bin."

Obi-Wan grinned. It was true; the food at the Learning Circle was terrible. All vegetables and meats were ground into a paste and then formed into round disks and cooked. The disks were so tasteless and tough that they could be used for shockball. He glanced at V-Davi to see if he had taken offense.

V-Davi's face was frozen in surprise, as if he'd never heard a joke before. Then he laughed. "The food is bad, yes. But it's not my fault. They tell me how to cook it."

"I wasn't blaming you, V-Davi," Siri told him. "You'd have to be a genius to come up with food this bad."

"At least I can help you finish cleaning up," V-Davi offered. "I don't mind."

"Don't worry about it," Siri told him as she finished mopping. "I got us into this. But you can tell us more about yourself while we work."

"How old were you when you came to the Learning Circle?" Obi-Wan asked.

"It was seven years ago. I was two years old," V-Davi said as he ran more vegetables through the grinder. "My parents died during the great Toli-X outbreak. I was sent here. Most children on Kegan don't start The Learning until they are four years old."

Siri exchanged a glance with Obi-Wan. Toli-X had been a deadly mutated virus that traveled through asteroid molds from world to world ten years before. A vaccine had been developed shortly after it had appeared. In other words, if Kegan had been in touch with other worlds in the galaxy, no one need have died.

Between them, a silent message was passed: *Don't tell him. Not if we don't have to.*

"Do you like living here?" Siri asked, turning to dry the dishes on the rack.

"Of course," V-Davi responded. "Thanks to The Learning, I am preparing how to best serve the General Good."

It sounded like one of the rote responses they had listened to in class. Obi-Wan helped Siri dry the tall stack of dishes. "Do you ever get to leave the Learning Circle?"

"When your course of study is complete," V-Davi said. "Usually around sixteen. But you know this."

"We aren't from here, V-Davi," Siri said. "O-Bin doesn't believe us, but it's true. Where do you go when you leave the Learning Circle?"

"Where the General Good is best served," V-Davi responded promptly. He scraped the vegetable mush into a big container and placed it in the cooler that ran along one wall. Then he began to carry the dried plates to the racks. "When you are twelve, you appear before a committee in which your aptitude is assessed. Then you receive more specialized training in your area."

"But what if you're assigned to something you don't want to do?" Siri asked.

"You are happy, because you know you are contributing to the General Good." V-Davi mopped up a bit more soapy water that Siri had spilled. He leaned against the sink and put his hand in his pocket nervously. "I'll probably go into food service. There is a shortage."

Siri gave him a shrewd glance. "What do you *want* to do, V-Davi?"

"I want to work in the Animal Circle," V-Davi

admitted. "But there is a surplus. So it wouldn't help the . . ."

"General Good," Siri completed. "I get it."

Suddenly, Obi-Wan heard a *peep peep.* Was it a warning security device? He looked around quickly, but could see no lights or indicators.

V-Davi looked nervous. "We'd better go."

Again, Obi-Wan heard the *peep peep.* He realized that it was coming from V-Davi's pocket.

"What's that?" Siri asked bluntly.

V-Davi moved toward the door. "Nothing. I must go. Lockdown is soon." He hurried away, and something floated through the air back toward Obi-Wan. He caught it. It was a feather.

"V-Davi," he called. "Stop."

V-Davi stopped.

"What are you holding?"

Siri walked forward. She peered into V-Davi's cupped hands. "It's a humming peeper."

Obi-Wan stepped forward. V-Davi must have been hiding the tiny bird in his pocket. It perched in his cupped hands, a lovely creature with bright yellow and blue feathers.

V-Davi's eyes darted fearfully from Obi-Wan to Siri. "It has a hurt wing. I found it in the yard. I was going to turn it in. I swear I was!"

Siri reached out a finger and stroked the bird. "He's cute."

"I-I just rescued this one creature," V-Davi stammered. "I would never break the rules of The Learning."

Suddenly, Obi-Wan saw a tiny quivering nose stick out of V-Davi's other pocket.

"And what's that?"

V-Davi's eyes were wide. "That's a baby ferbil," he whispered. "Please don't turn me in, V-Obi."

"Of course we won't turn you in," Obi-Wan assured him. He stroked the furry creature's head.

"Is having pets against the rules?" Siri asked.

"Of course. There are no domestic pets allowed on Kegan," V-Davi said. "It is contrary to the General Good to lavish attention on a subspecies. They are used for food products and cultivation only." His gray eyes studied them, suddenly fearful. "You *are* outsiders, aren't you?"

"Yes," Siri said. "But we're also your friends."

A relieved smile spread over V-Davi's face. "Students of The Learning are not encouraged to form personal attachments. If you make a close friend, you find he or she is moved to another Learning quad. So we must be careful. But you must call me Davi now. When one forms a bond on Kegan, the title letter of your name is dropped."

"Then you can call us Obi-Wan and Siri," Obi-Wan said.

Davi reached out and put one hand on Obi-Wan's forearm and one on Siri's. "You are my first friends. Maybe it does not add to the General Good. But I am happy. Now, since you are my friends, on Kegan we believe in trying to help our bonded friends achieve their hearts desire." He took a deep breath. "Therefore, Obi and Siri, I will help you escape. Tonight."

CHAPTER 10

The constant buzzing noise should have alerted him. Instead, it had become background, and Qui-Gon had ceased to notice it. That was what they counted on, he supposed. A constant presence can be easier to ignore than a random one.

There was complete surveillance on Kegan. The skyhoppers overhead had to be equipped with listening and watching devices. It was the only explanation.

V-Nen and O-Melie had asked for their help in the only way available to them: with glances and hints.

Qui-Gon and Adi did not dare speak, even in the open air. Without another word, they started toward the Communications Circle.

Qui-Gon's keen gaze swept across the round buildings in the Circle. He saw one open window in the building to his left. He indicated it to Adi with a tilt of his head. She nodded.

They walked into the building and quickly made their way through a maze of corridors toward the room with the open window. They were sure V-Nen and O-Melie would be waiting.

The door was slightly ajar. Qui-Gon hesitated outside.

"Come in quickly please," V-Nen whispered.

"And please close the door," O-Melie added.

"This is a safe room," V-Nen said as soon as the Jedi entered and shut the door behind them. "Melie and I have installed anti-surveillance devices. The skyhoppers you may have noticed overhead are actually unpiloted auto-hoppers that contain audio and visual surveillance devices. Everything we say and do is recorded. There are transmitters in our homes that beam up to them."

Qui-Gon and Adi exchanged glances. "We thought that might be the case," Qui-Gon said. "How did the citizens of Kegan allow this?"

"It began as an anti-crime measure," O-Melie explained. "Society was stable, but petty theft and pilfering was common after we changed to a bartering system. V-Tan and O-Vieve proposed we use autohoppers as security devices, and we all voted on it. Originally they were supposed to patrol the market only. Then it was extended to the Dwelling Circle and beyond. No one expected that it would be used to monitor conversations and activities. It happened slowly, and now we are watched all the time."

"But if every citizen on Kegan gets a vote, couldn't you vote them out?" Adi asked.

V-Nen shook his head. "Every citizen gets a vote, but V-Tan and O-Vieve decide what we should vote on."

O-Melie gave a sad smile. "We have the illusion of democracy. Not the reality."

"Tell us how we can help you," Adi said gently. "What do you think happened to O-Lana?"

O-Melie and V-Nen exchanged a frightened glance. "We are worried about her safety," V-Nen said quietly. "There are whispers and rumors about children who vanish."

Qui-Gon recalled something that had bothered him at the time. "Is that what O-Yani meant when she said O-Lana would not *disappear*?"

O-Melie nodded. "Some children enroll at the Learning Circle and are never heard from again."

"The Learning Circle?" Qui-Gon asked quickly. "Where is that?"

"That Circle is not in the city of Kegan, but in an outlying area," V-Nen explained. "The

Learning is a course of teaching developed by O-Vieve and V-Tan. It was introduced about fifteen years ago. Before that there was no central authority and children were schooled at home."

"We don't know where it is, only that it is in the open country," O-Melie answered. "It is thought better for the children if parents are not allowed there. Children attend the Learning Circle from the age of four. There are no exceptions. Truants are dealt with harshly."

"That's why there are no children on the streets," Adi said.

"Obi-Wan and Siri!" Qui-Gon exclaimed. "Could they have been taken there by mistake?"

"It's possible," V-Nen said. "We hear that the Truant Guides take action first and ask questions later. And they might not believe your Padawans if they say they are not from Kegan. There are very few citizens who know the Jedi are here. O-Vieve and V-Tan thought it best if your arrival was kept secret."

"You see, we contacted you without V-Tan and O-Vieve's permission," O-Melie said. "We took the chance that our Benevolent Guides would not dare refuse the Jedi. They did not. They allowed you to come. But they would not let us see you alone."

"They claim it is for our protection," V-Nen

told them. "They believe that darkness surrounds the Jedi."

Qui-Gon was startled. "I don't understand."

"O-Vieve has prophetic visions," O-Melie explained. "V-Tan has dreams. Many of their predictions have come true. That is why the people of Kegan trust them. O-Vieve had a vision of the Jedi. She claims that an evil force will engulf those who are close to the Jedi. All Keganites are afraid of the Jedi."

So Adi was right. That was what she had picked up from V-Haad and O-Rina. Fear.

"But we doubt O-Vieve's vision," V-Nen said. "We want what's best for our daughter. We had to contact you. We know Lana wasn't taken for routine testing. We would have heard something by now."

A sob broke loose from O-Melie.

V-Nen put his arm protectively around his wife. He laid his hand on her hair, holding her head against him gently. He spoke with his cheek resting against her hair. "I'm sorry to say these things out loud, Melie, but I know you are thinking them, too. We must be strong for Lana's sake. We must allow the Jedi to help us. We can't do it alone."

Slowly, O-Melie raised her head. Tears sparkled in her eyes. "Nen is right," she said shakily. "We need your help."

"And we are here to give it," Qui-Gon said.

V-Nen put his hand on Qui-Gon's forearm. O-Melie put hers on Adi Gallia's.

V-Nen said, "Now we are Nen and Melie to you. Our fate is twined with yours."

"We will find your daughter," Qui-Gon assured them.

"You must be careful," Nen told them. "We are part of a faction on Kegan that opposes O-Vieve and V-Tan. We believe that the isolation policy is wrong. Trade and exploration could be good for Kegan. The surveillance is what has made our anti-isolationist movement so difficult. It's not that we are arrested or forbidden to discuss things — on the contrary, V-Tan and O-Vieve insist that Kegan is an open society. Yet somehow those of us who ask why we cannot travel beyond Kegan are punished — moved to job sectors we do not like, forced to share housing unexpectedly, given low priority for requests . . . things that make life difficult on Kegan. You may imagine that the movement has thus lost many members. The rest have learned to be careful."

"But now they have gone too far. They have taken our daughter," Melie said. "I do not want to be careful any longer."

"V-Tan and O-Vieve have said that if one Keganite leaves the planet it will cause our destruction," Nen continued. "They will prevent Lana leaving in whatever way they can."

"We must find her before it's too late," Melie said, her voice trembling.

"Yet every move is watched. Every word we say is heard," Nen added in despair.

"I have an idea," Qui-Gon said. "Auto-hoppers are controlled by CIPs — Central Instruction Processors."

"Yes," Nen agreed. "The CIP is in a guarded building right here in the Comm Circle."

"If Adi and I can disable the CIP, they will need to recall the autohoppers until it is repaired. In the meantime, the people will be able to share information more freely. You will be able to mobilize your group, and we will have time to search for Lana."

"Qui-Gon, I must speak to you," Adi said sternly.

She drew Qui-Gon into the corner.

"I must object to this plan," she said in a low tone that vibrated with worry. "It is totally opposed to the Council's wishes. We will directly interfere with the Kegan government if we disable a CIP."

"But how else can we complete our mission?" Qui-Gon argued. "We didn't know before we arrived that the people here were under constant surveillance. We didn't know that two powerful rulers were controlling them. And our Padawans and an innocent child weren't missing!"

Adi pressed her lips together. She cast her eyes on the floor, thinking.

"Adi, we must find them," Qui-Gon said softly. "This is the only way."

Adi raised her head. Her deep brown eyes still were clouded by doubt. She did not speak.

"I understand if you don't wish to help me," Qui-Gon said firmly. "But I will disable that CIP. The question is, will you come with me?"

CHAPTER 11

Davi, Obi-Wan, and Siri sat in a dark corner of the food hall.

"What are we waiting for?" Siri whispered to Davi.

"Lockdown," Davi said. "The lights will go on and off three times. The Security Guides will change shifts. V-Tarz is on tonight. He'll sit at the surveillance post in the admin center. If anyone steps foot out of the dorm quads, an alarm will sound."

"So how will we escape?" Siri asked.

"V-Tarz waits five minutes after lockdown, then turns off security in Quad 7 and raids the kitchen," Davi said with a grin. "I found this out the night I met Scurry." He placed the ferbil on his palm and fed it a few seeds. "Scurry was in the food prep area. He must have gotten in somehow and couldn't find his way out. I knew if they found him he'd be . . . gotten rid of. I was trying to figure out how to keep him when the lockdown warning came. I decided to spend the night where I was. It's six punishment marks if you're caught out after lockdown. V-Tarz came in for a snack, so I hid."

"How do you know he does it every night?" Obi-Wan asked.

"Because you can see the security light blink off in the dorm," Davi explained. "I come out here almost every night. Sometimes I'm . . . I'm afraid to be alone in the dark."

"But you sleep in a room with twenty other boys," Obi-Wan said.

"I'm still alone," Davi said. Embarrassed, he looked down quickly to pet the ferbil.

"Listen, I know what you mean," Siri said bluntly. "This place could give anyone the wild shivers."

Davi looked up with a shy smile. Once again, Siri's forthright manner had reassured him, Obi-Wan noted. He would never have imagined that Siri was capable of comforting anyone.

"Scurry helps," Davi said. "And my other pets. I find them in the yard during rec period. Most of them are hungry or scared or hurt. I smuggle them in and keep them by my bed. At night I sneak in here to get food for them. Sometimes I sneak outside just to see the stars."

"How do we get out?" Obi-Wan asked.

"Through the windows in the cleansing room of Quad 7," Davi said. "You can use the shower heads to swing up. It's an easy drop to the ground. Then you'll have to steal a landspeeder. I can give you the coordinates of the city."

The lights turned on and off three times. A soft signal sounded.

"In another five minutes, the floor will be alarmed," Davi whispered. "But then V-Tarz will turn it off again. I'll show you the way."

"Why don't you come with us, Davi?" Siri asked.

Davi shrank back. "Why would I do that?"

"Don't you want to find out what's really happening in the galaxy?" Siri asked. "Don't you want a chance to do what you want to do?"

"But the galaxy is a dangerous place," Davi said.

"Some of it is dangerous," Obi-Wan said. "Not all."

"There are places on Coruscant, where we live, that place orphan children with parents," Siri told him. "You could have a family. You could keep pets and work with animals."

"I *have* a family," Davi said nervously. "The General Good is a family."

"But Davi, The Learning is telling you lies," Siri said. "Don't you trust us?"

"It's not that I don't trust you," Davi said worriedly. "But the power of evil that controls the galaxy might be telling you things that aren't true. Misinformation is spread to confuse the people and keep them in line."

"But that's exactly what's happening *here*," Siri protested.

"If I leave, the Masked Soldiers will come and attack Kegan," Davi said, shaking his head. "This is the vision of O-Vieve and V-Tan. No one must leave. The General Good will suffer, and invaders will come."

Siri and Obi-Wan exchanged a frustrated glance. Davi had been trained in The Learning for too long. He could not accept what they told him as true.

They heard the heavy tread of V-Tarz. The massive Keganite moved through the food hall, heading for the kitchens. Obi-Wan stayed perfectly still. In only a few minutes, he and Siri would be free.

If everything went according to plan . . .

A voice suddenly split the silence. "V-Tarz!"

Another Security Guide stood in the doorway. "What are you doing?"

"Security alert in the kitchens," V-Tarz said quickly. "Probably just a malfunction. Maybe the infrared alarm. I was just checking it out."

"I'll go with you. New orders are for two posted guards during the lockdown hours. We'd better get Quad 7 back online quickly." The other Guide moved toward V-Tarz.

"There goes V-Tarz's snack," Siri murmured.

"We'd better get back to our dorm quarters," Davi said nervously. "We won't be able to escape tonight. I'm sorry. They've never put two guards on at night before."

They waited until the Guides had turned the corner. Then Davi led them out of the food hall.

"We can get back to the dorms through the admin center," Davi said. "Hurry, it won't take them long to check out the kitchen security."

They raced through the halls and entered the admin center, a round room that was in the center of the building. All the different quads spun off from this central location.

"Almost there," Davi said as he hurried toward the door that led to the Quad 7 dorm, where they were all quartered.

But just then they heard familiar footsteps behind them. There wasn't enough time to make it to the door. Quickly, Davi sprang behind a row of desks. Siri hurried after him. Obi-Wan was bringing up the rear. He slipped behind a wall of shelves that held data files.

They could hear V-Tarz grumbling as he moved toward the security wall.

"Run the infrared check, he says," he muttered. "There's nothing wrong with the infrared. What's wrong is that I'm starving."

"V-Tarz? Are you there?" The voice came through the comlink on the console.

"I'm here."

"Run check."

"Running," V-Tarz said. "You idiot."

"What?"

"Nothing. Running check." V-Tarz's stomach rumbled. He sighed.

Obi-Wan leaned against the console to peer around it. Would they be able to slip past V-Tarz? Not if he didn't move. V-Tarz had a perfect view of the door they needed to pass through.

As Obi-Wan retreated back behind the shelves, he brushed against a container that was overstuffed with data files. One of them slipped off the top. Obi-Wan's reflexes were excellent, and he caught it soundlessly.

It was a file for someone named O-Uni. Obi-Wan leafed through it quietly. The girl had excellent reports from her teachers. A few visits to the med circle. Then a paper stamped RECLASSIFIED TO RE-LEARNING CIRCLE.

Obi-Wan carefully replaced the file. The Re-Learning Circle? What was that?

"Check complete," V-Tarz said into the comlink. "No problems."

"Copy that. Making one last check of kitchen and food hall before I get back."

"I'll give you a hand."

"Don't bother. I've got it covered."

"Didn't copy that. I'll check the kitchen." V-Tarz switched off the comlink. "Maybe I can sneak some veg patties when you're not looking, killjoy."

He lumbered off. Davi immediately poked his head out.

"Let's go," he hissed.

They hurried toward the door, but Obi-Wan stopped Davi for a moment. "What's the Re-Learning Circle?"

"I'm not sure," Davi said. "But I know I don't want to end up there. You get sent there if you have enough punishment marks. But then some kids who are never in trouble get sent there, too. Nobody knows why." He shuddered. "But nobody ever comes back."

CHAPTER 12

The morning gong shattered the silence before dawn. Instantly, students threw back their covers and stood, lining up to use the wash basins that ran along the wall.

Obi-Wan felt the shock of cold water against his skin. His mind was already clear. The next gong sounded, the signal to dress and proceed to the food hall within three minutes. Davi had explained what was required last night before they'd separated.

Obi-Wan reflected how different life at the Temple had been. There, a soft light began slowly and grew in brightness, mimicking a rising sun. The students all had their own quarters, as privacy was respected. Early morning was a time of meditation and gentle exercise before the day began. It was not harsh noise and hurry.

Here the students did not seem to mind the

abrupt start of the day or the strict schedule they had to follow. They did not seem to notice the contrast between the smiles of the Guides and their sharp orders. And nobody seemed to mind the food.

Across the room, Siri sat with the other girls. She lifted a spoonful of grain mash and made a face at him. Obi-Wan laughed quietly to himself.

"Two punishments marks, V-Obi," one of the Guides said, entering it into a touch pad. "Concentration on nutrition is what we do during meal service. Interaction with others is saved for free time."

Obi-Wan chewed on the tasteless meal. Siri was right. They had to get out of here.

"Today we will play Response Time," O-Bin announced. "You all know how this is done. A topic will flash on your screen. Whoever hits their response button first will tell the class what the significant facts about the topic are. Good luck."

Obi-Wan glanced at his data screen. CORUSCANT flashed across it. He did not hit his response button. The best thing he could do today was try not to attract any attention from the Teaching Guides.

Jedi responses are lightning fast. The light on

top of Siri's data screen lit up first. Obi-Wan threw her a warning glance, but she ignored it.

O-Bin was clearly not pleased at having to call on Siri. "O-Siri?" she asked through pursed lips.

"Coruscant is a world made up of one city. It is the home of the Galactic Senate. Billions of beings live on Coruscant. It is known for government and culture and its excellent transit and security systems —"

"I must interrupt you, O-Siri," O-Bin said with a smile. "That is all wrong. Can anyone correct O-Siri?"

Data screen lights glowed throughout the classroom. O-Bin consulted her screen to see who had been first. "V-Mina?"

"Coruscant is a world of corruption," V-Mina said. "Slavery is legal there."

"Precisely," O-Bin said.

Siri's face was burning. Obi-Wan fixed her with a steady gaze. They both had to keep quiet. They should not attract any more attention.

JEDI ORDER.

This time, O-Bin deliberately ignored Siri's glowing light. "V-Taun?"

"The Jedi Order is surrounded by darkness. They —"

Siri sprang to her feet. "The Jedi path is one of service to the galaxy!"

"Sit down, O-Siri! Five punishment marks! And you know what that means . . ."

Obi-Wan groaned loudly.

"Food service cleanup after the evening meal," O-Bin hissed through her teeth. "And V-Obi, from your groan I'm sure you'll be happy to join O-Siri. So much better for the General Good."

"I *am* capable of keeping my mouth shut," Siri told Obi-Wan later. "I just don't want to. What difference does it make if we're washing dishes? At least we're not sitting in a class listening to O-Bin tell us that the Core Worlds are corrupted."

Obi-Wan regarded the stack of dishes crusted with the remains of the evening meal. It was the second time they had been given cleanup duty that day. "I think I'd rather be sitting in class."

"I have a suggestion." Siri threw the dishrag into the sink. "Let's forget the dishes and escape. Tonight. If we can't outsmart that greedy V-Tarz, we don't deserve to be Jedi."

"All right," he agreed.

"Obi-Wan, you've got to listen to me sometime. You're not the only one who can —" Siri did a double take. "Did you just agree with me?"

Obi-Wan nodded. "You're right. We saw how the security system operates. Let's do it. Qui-Gon and Adi must be really worried now."

"There will be two guards," Siri said. "And V-Tarz might not be able to go for his snack. What do you have in mind?"

"The other Security Guide thinks the system malfunctioned last night, but they don't know where the problem is, right?"

Siri nodded.

"So let's create a real problem," Obi-Wan said. "They'll have to shut down the system to check and repair it. Meanwhile we'll sneak out the cleansing room window."

"How can we sabotage the system?" Siri asked. "We can't sneak into the admin center now. It's full of Guides."

"We have to sabotage it here," Obi-Wan said, glancing around the kitchen. "Any ideas?"

They examined the security devices set into the ceiling corners.

"Didn't V-Tarz say something about the in-frared sensor?" Siri asked.

"He claimed that it could be malfunctioning," Obi-Wan said.

"Can we rig something to set it off again?" Siri asked. She ran her hand along the big warming unit. "What if we turned the stoves on low? They'd heat the room and eventually the infrareds would go off. They'd have to turn off the system to figure it out."

"Simple, but genius," Obi-Wan said. "Let's do it. But we'd better wash the dishes first. If a Guide comes in to check our work, he or she might notice the stoves are on."

"I knew there was a drawback," Siri groaned.

Working quickly, the two finished their task. The warning lights flashed for lockdown, and they ran for their dorm quarters. They paused outside the admin center.

"We don't have time to say good-bye to Davi," Siri said in concern.

"He'll know what happened when he finds out we're gone. We can come back for him with Qui-Gon and Adi. Meet me here as soon as the security light goes out," Obi-Wan said. "Then we'll head for the Quad 7 exit."

Siri nodded. Obi-Wan headed to his dorm quarters. He managed to slip into bed just before the lights went out. He waited, listening to the breathing slow around him. The students worked so hard and long during the day that everyone fell deeply asleep within minutes of lying down.

At last the security light blinked off. Obi-Wan slipped into his boots and tiptoed out. He hesitated near Davi's sleep couch. It was better not to awaken him. Anything could go wrong, and he didn't want to get Davi in trouble.

When he reached the hall outside the admin center, Siri was waiting.

"I just saw V-Tarz and the other Security Guide take off to check that sensor," she said. "It's an all clear."

They hurried down the long hallway, past the other dorm rooms. The cleansing room was at the very end of the long, circular building. They had almost reached it when they heard the scrape of a door opening slightly.

Without hesitating a fraction, Obi-Wan and Siri leaped together toward the curve of the hallway, where they would be out of sight. They hit the floor and began to run. If someone had caught a glimpse of them, or even merely heard them, Security Guides might be called. Each student was encouraged to inform on the others.

But would they?

An alarm pierced the silence. The door to the cleansing room was in sight. They raced toward it. But before they could reach it, Security Guides spilled out into the hallway and surrounded them.

They could have fought them. But that meant they would have to draw their lightsabers. Obi-Wan was still reluctant to do that, since Yoda had cautioned them against it. There had to be a better way. He saw Siri's hand drift to her lightsaber hilt, and he shook his head. But would Siri listen to him?

Students spilled out into the hall to see what had caused the disturbance. O-Bin and several other Teaching Guides hurried out, dressed in their sleepwear.

"I know these two well," O-Bin said. "What are you doing out in the hallways after curfew?"

A shaky voice came from behind them. "It was me."

They turned. Davi stood nervously, his eyes on the floor, afraid to look at O-Bin.

"I was heading for the food prep area," Davi said. "I . . . forgot something."

"I'll say he did!" V-Tarz hurried forward. "He left all the stoves on! Tripped the sensors!"

O-Bin plastered her chiding smile on her face. "This is very careless of you, V-Davi. We will have to consult to figure out how many punishment marks you will receive."

"I know," Davi mumbled. "I realize that I endangered the General Good. I am repentant."

"Well. We shall discuss this tomorrow." O-Bin clapped her hands. "Everyone return to your quarters."

Amid the crush of students, Obi-Wan and Siri made their way to Davi.

"Why did you do that?" Siri whispered.

"I don't have as many punishment marks as you," Davi whispered back.

"Davi, why are you wearing your boots and outer tunic?" Obi-Wan asked shrewdly.

"I saw you leave," Davi said. "I knew you were going to escape. I wanted to come with you!"

"V-Davi!" O-Bin's voice was shrill. "If you want to repent for your disobedience, you should not be talking to two troublemakers!"

With a last glance at them, Davi backed up. But suddenly something shot out of his pocket. Obi-Wan knew immediately what it was: Davi's pet ferbil, Scurry. Davi would not leave the Learning Circle without his pet.

"What is that?" O-Bin snapped. "Catch it!"

Davi went down on his hands and knees. He made a chirping noise with his mouth and cupped his hands. The ferbil ran into his palm.

"That," O-Bin said, "is a pet."

Davi said nothing. His face flamed.

"It's just a little ferbil," Siri said.

"Two punishment marks, O-Siri. I was not talking to you. V-Tarz!"

V-Tarz rumbled forward. "Please search V-Davi's dorm area," O-Bin ordered.

Obi-Wan and Siri followed. While the students stood around, it did not take V-Tarz long to find two iridescent lizards, another baby ferbil, and a bag of seeds.

O-Bin pressed her lips together. "What do we say, students?"

All the students faced Davi.

"SHAME. SHAME. SHAME," they repeated over and over.

"Take . . . those . . . things," O-Bin told V-Tarz, her teeth clenched in a smile. "And get rid of them."

V-Tarz scooped up the lizards and put both ferbils in his pocket.

"No!" Davi cried. "Please . . ."

"SHAME. SHAME. SHAME."

Inside V-Tarz's pocket, the ferbils chirped anxiously.

Davi's eyes filled. Tears slowly dripped down his cheeks. "Please," he whispered.

As soon as the lights powered up the next morning, Obi-Wan hurried to Davi's sleep couch to give him words of encouragement. They would find a way out. They would take him with them.

But Davi was gone.

CHAPTER 13

Qui-Gon and Adi hid behind a low wall, their eyes on the high security building that housed the CIP. Nen had brought them through several checkpoints, but he was not authorized to enter the building. It was up to them to get past the guards.

"We cannot attack any Keganite," Adi murmured. "We must use the Force to bypass security."

"There is only one guard," Qui-Gon said. "It should be easy. Kegan is not used to unlawful activity."

They rose from their hiding place and strolled toward the guard.

"Greetings," Qui-Gon said. "V-Tan and O-Vieve have sent us here to observe. You will be happy to let us pass through."

"I am happy to let you pass through," the

guard said, succumbing to the mind trick and waving them through the doorway.

Once they were inside, Qui-Gon and Adi quickly found the Central Instruction Processor. Adi's fingers flew at the keyboard as she entered a series of contradictory instructions.

"This should send them all to landing sites," she said. "I don't want them to crash in a populated area. This program should confuse the tech personnel and give us time."

"How long?" Qui-Gon asked.

Adi's eyes never left the data screen. "Hard to say. It should give us at least two hours. Maybe three. They aren't technologically advanced, so it could take them a while."

"I don't want another night to fall without finding our Padawans," Qui-Gon said grimly.

Adi agreed quietly. "We will find them. And Lana, too."

When Adi was finished, they turned toward the exit hallway, but Qui-Gon stopped by a door marked CENTRAL INSTRUCTION FILE RECORDS.

"Let's just look in here a minute," he said. "We could find a clue."

The room was lined with holographic file units. They were dated and lined up alphabetically. Qui-Gon accessed a drawer of files, Adi another.

"There's a file on every citizen of Kegan

here," Adi Gallia said in disbelief. "Recorded conversations . . ."

"Whom they meet, whom they dine with . . ." Qui-Gon said, accessing another file.

"What they use, what they eat . . ."

"What they write to their children at school . . ."

Qui-Gon studied a file for a thirteen-year-old named O-Nena. "Didn't Nen tell us about The Learning Circle?"

Adi Gallia murmured assent as she accessed another file. "Did you find out where it is?"

"No," Qui-Gon said. "But here's a reference to a *Re*-Learning Circle. What could that be?"

"Sounds like something to check out."

"Let's look up Lana," Qui-Gon suggested, flicking past files to get to her name. "There's nothing here."

"I'll try Melie and Nen." Adi searched through the files, flashing one name after another. "Here. I'll take Nen, you take Melie." She read through the files quickly.

Qui-Gon scanned the file. "Plenty of recorded conversations. Records of meetings with other dissidents. And record of all our conversations in their house. But nothing about Lana. Not even the recording of her birth."

"They've erased all the information." Adi met Qui-Gon's gaze. "I don't like this. It's as though they wiped out any evidence of her existence."

"Except in her parents' memories."

Simultaneously, the two Jedi closed the files.

"There's no time to lose," Adi said.

They left the building and hurried to Nen and Melie's dwelling. Adi quickly explained that the autohoppers would be grounded for about three hours.

"We'll gather as many dissidents as we can," Nen said. "We'll try to find out if anyone has seen your Padawans."

"We must find out where the Learning Circle is located," Qui-Gon told them. "I have a feeling the key is there. Have you ever heard of the Re-Learning Circle?"

"I've heard it mentioned," Nen said. "Nobody really knows what it is. Some sort of training facility."

"The mothers talk," Melie said. "They say if your child is reassigned they are not allowed to contact you again. Do you think that's where Lana is?"

O-Yani, the elder caregiver, stood in the doorway. "No," she whispered.

Melie turned, her gaze suddenly sharp. "O-Yani, your grandson V-Onin was sent to the Re-Learning Circle six years ago."

"It was not my fault he was ill," O-Yani said quickly.

"I know," Melie said gently. "I saw how you cared for him. Why was he taken away?"

"For the General Good," O-Yani said promptly.

"O-Yani, we have disabled the autohoppers," Qui-Gon said to her. "You don't hear them flying, do you? You can speak freely."

O-Yani paused. She looked out the window, waiting for the sight or sound of the autohoppers. "They gave me this job. I like working with children," she said wistfully.

"You won't lose your job," Nen told her. "We know that what happened to Lana wasn't your fault."

"But if you know where she is, please tell us," Melie said.

"The medics didn't know how to treat V-Onin. They said they had a place for him to go . . . a place where research was done. What could we do?" O-Yani's face was bleak. "I never saw him again."

"Do you know where they took him?" Melie pressed.

"A trader came one day and knocked on my door," O-Yani said. "He had seen a boy in the country who was traveling with Guides. The Guides had trouble with their airspeeder and were repairing it. The boy stopped the trader.

He gave him something to bring to me. A good-bye gift."

"What was it?" Nen asked.

"Wildflowers," O-Yani said. "I pressed them in a book. Wait."

She disappeared and came out a moment later with a leather-bound book. She cracked it open and carefully extracted a delicate, pressed bloom.

"May I see it?" Melie asked respectfully. At O-Yani's hesitant nod, she plucked it from her hand and examined it. "I know this bloom. It comes off the calla tree. They only grow on the highest plateau of Kegan. It's about two hours away by landspeeder."

Thanks to the Jedi's faster craft, they could cut that amount of time in less than half, Qui-Gon calculated. "How big is the plateau itself?" he asked.

"You could cover it in a matter of minutes with the right craft and surveillance devices," Melie answered. "It's not very large."

"Let's go," Qui-Gon said to Adi.

Suddenly the door flew open. Six Enforcement Guides stormed into the room.

"Qui-Gon Jinn and Adi Gallia, we are here to escort you to the High Court. You have been found guilty of mind control. Come quietly or you will be shot."

CHAPTER 14

Siri used the bustle of departure from the food hall to drift close to Obi-Wan.

"Davi was taken to The Re-Learning Circle," she told him in a low voice. "I overheard O-Bin talking to another Teaching Guide. We've got to do something."

"I thought you wanted to escape," Obi-Wan said.

Siri bit her lip. "Not until we find Davi."

"I feel the same way," Obi-Wan agreed.

"I think the Re-Learning Circle is right here, in the Learning Circle itself," Siri told him.

"We have rec time today. Let's try to sneak away and explore then," Obi-Wan suggested. "Just don't cause trouble in class, or we'll have cleanup duty instead."

Siri nodded. They walked in orderly rows to class. The morning stretched on. Often O-Bin would glance at Siri during the lesson, waiting for her objection. But Siri remained silent, her face serene. Obi-Wan could feel members of the class wondering if O-Bin had won the battle and subdued her.

At last, classes ended and the students filed outdoors. Rec time consisted of running along a track that spanned a good part of the Learning Circle. Along the track various stations were set up for exercises that tested balance, coordination, and strength. They did not race against one other but against their own former times. Each student wore a sensor that recorded his or her progress after every lap. The sensors were connected to a large readout screen. The goal was to complete five circuits. Then they would be free to stroll around the part of the Circle set apart for outdoor activities.

Several classes ran the course at the same time. Teaching Guides supervised them, but they were more interested in drinking in the sun or talking among themselves than patrolling the students.

"Let's run the course as fast as we can," Obi-Wan suggested. "The sooner our five scores are recorded, the more free time we'll have."

Obi-Wan and Siri ran easily side by side. Within seconds, they were ahead of the pack. They reached the first station, a narrow beam suspended several meters above the ground.

The beam curved in a twisting shape in order to test balance. Without breaking stride, Siri, then Obi-Wan, leaped up on it, landed without wavering even a fraction, and lightly ran through its twists and turns without a pause. Siri leaped off the end, somersaulted, and landed. Obi-Wan followed her lead.

The next station was a durasteel wall that had small handholds and footholds to aid climbing. It glistened in the sun.

"I think it's coated to make it more slippery," Obi-Wan said to Siri as he raced alongside her. "Might be tricky to climb."

She grinned. "Why bother?"

Using the Force, Siri leaped and landed on top of the wall, then sprang off and flew through the air. Again, Obi-Wan followed. He landed on top of the wall and jumped down easily.

They were far ahead now. The track course was an easy exercise for them. They had been studying balance and coordination at the Temple from an early age. They rounded the first lap and their score was recorded. Soon they outran others still on their first lap.

Around and around Siri and Obi-Wan ran. Students flooded the course, the faster ones in their second lap, the slower still on the first. It was easy to lose themselves in the crowd.

When they completed the fifth lap, they jogged easily along until they got to a part of the course that curved away from where the Teaching Guides sat on benches, enjoying the sun. Then they simply strolled away.

They noted utility sheds, more classrooms, Security Guide outposts, sleeping quarters for workers, supply sheds, and a landing platform. Nowhere did they see a building that could be the Re-Learning Circle.

"Maybe I was wrong," Siri said, discouraged. "But O-Bin clearly said that Davi packed his belongings and V-Tarz walked him there. They didn't take a speeder."

"We've covered most of the compound," Obi-Wan said. "The rest is just cultivated gardens and fields for food production."

Siri gazed over the fields. "Is quinto grain valuable on Kegan?" she asked.

"Not especially," Obi-Wan said. "It's Kegan's basic crop. It's the base for those veg patties that you love so much."

"If it's not valuable, why are ten Security Guides guarding it?" Siri asked.

Obi-Wan looked in the distance. Siri's sharp eyes had noted the Guides lined up in a field.

"Let's get closer," he suggested.

Using the field of grain as cover, they moved toward the Guides. When they got closer, they took out electrobinoculars from their utility belts.

The Guides stood ten paces apart. They looked bored. One of them yawned. Another stamped his feet.

"I don't see anything unusual," Siri said.

"Look at the dirt near the third guard, the one who stamped his feet," Obi-Wan said.

Siri trained her electrobinoculars on the loose dirt that had been disturbed. "Something is buried there," she said excitedly. "I see metal."

"Hold on," Obi-Wan said. The ground was moving. The guard stepped quickly away as a panel slid open and a ramp leading downward was revealed.

A Kegan woman emerged, wearing the white tunic of a medic. The door closed behind her and she hurried down the path in the direction of the Med Dome.

"That's got to be it," Siri said. "But how can we break in? We have to find a way to activate that ramp."

"I know how to get in," Obi-Wan said. "It's all up to you. And it will be easy."

"Me? How?" Siri asked warily.

He grinned. "Just do what comes naturally."

CHAPTER 15

Qui-Gon and Adi stood in the center of the coliseum. Opposite them was a circular table full of Keganites in red tunics. They were Judgment Guides.

"You have been found guilty of mind control in the case of O-Melie and V-Nen," an elder Keganite said. "The penalty is deportation. Your ship is fueled and ready. Escort starfighters will accompany you to the outer atmosphere."

Qui-Gon and Adi said nothing. They knew that V-Tan and O-Vieve were behind this. It would be wasted effort to argue. But that did not mean they would submit.

They were led to the landing platform by a platoon of Security Guides.

One of them spoke. "We have taken the liberty of disabling all weapons and defense systems. We wish you good travel."

A door hissed open, and V-Tan and O-Vieve appeared. They walked toward the Jedi, kind smiles on their faces.

"Before you leave, we wish to assure you that we mean you no harm," O-Vieve said.

"Where are our Padawans?" Qui-Gon asked.

"We think they were taken in a Truant Sweep," V-Tan answered. "We will locate them at the Learning Circle and send them back to Coruscant. We give you our personal assurance that this will be so."

"I'm sorry, that isn't good enough," Qui-Gon answered politely.

"You do not trust us. Yet you should." O-Vieve leaned closer to Qui-Gon and touched his shoulder reassuringly. Suddenly, her face drained of color. Even her bright blue eyes seemed to fade. She weaved unsteadily.

"Are you all right?" Qui-Gon asked, touching her hand. It was ice-cold.

O-Vieve dropped her hand from Qui-Gon's shoulder. "It is nothing. Sometimes I see things. They come without warning. This is why we've done what we have done. We only serve to protect our people."

"We agreed to your coming with friendship in our hearts," V-Tan said. "What we cannot tolerate is interference in our affairs. It disrupts the

General Good. You pushed the limits of what we were willing to give. Kegan is not interested in other worlds. We want to be left alone."

"You told the people that if one person left Kegan, the planet would be destroyed," Adi said. "Surely you don't believe that."

"But we do," O-Vieve said gently. "I have seen it."

"We understand your concern," Qui-Gon said. "And we recognize your right to evict us. But you must know that if you force us to leave without our Padawans, we will return with an investigative team from the Galactic Senate. Kegan will no longer be able to isolate itself."

V-Tan and O-Vieve exchanged a nervous glance.

O-Vieve tucked her hands into the wide sleeves of her white tunic. "If you would indulge us, kind Jedi, and listen. I have seen visions of the future since I was a little girl. V-Tan has dreams in which he sees things, too. When we met each other, we discovered that our visions matched. That convinced us of the truth of them. We have predicted things that have taken place. Now we see an invasion of evil on Kegan. We created a way of living that might avoid what we see."

"Everything we have done is to protect our citizens from a fate they cannot imagine," V-Tan said. "Perhaps some of our measures seem harsh, but they are only for the General Good."

"We have both seen flashes of a future destructive event on Kegan," O-Vieve told them. "We see evil cloaking our planet like a black cloud."

"How?" Qui-Gon asked. "When?"

"We do not know the answers to those questions," O-Vieve said. "That is the agony we live with. We are not sure how to prevent it. We only have clues. The Jedi . . . the Jedi are involved."

"The Jedi?" Adi asked. "How?"

"We see the Jedi surrounded by darkness," V-Tan said. "That is all we know. The darkness comes from within them and then spreads to engulf them."

"Perhaps our destruction will come from an explosive device sent to destroy an entire planet without a shiver," O-Vieve said.

"There is no explosive device powerful enough to destroy a whole planet," Qui-Gon said.

"Not yet, perhaps," O-Vieve corrected softly, and Qui-Gon felt a shiver go up his spine.

"We see masked soldiers," V-Tan said. "We do not know who they are, or what they want. Only that they are evil. They will bring fear and suffering."

"But your visions could be wrong," Adi said.

"Visions sometimes are. The Jedi themselves are not unused to them. Yet we recognize that we can only see things that *may* be."

"That is why we act as we do." O-Vieve looked at Qui-Gon with an intense gaze. "If you could choose your death, Qui-Gon, wouldn't you rather die in peace and comfort than violently in battle, in shock and despair?"

Qui-Gon fixed her with an icy stare. "We are not allowed to choose our deaths."

"And it is not up to you to choose what is best for your people," Adi said. "You say that each citizen has a vote. Yet you control the process. You monitor their thoughts and conversations. All because of a vision that may not come to pass. Is that fair? Is it fair to take a child from her parents based on a dream of an unnamed evil?"

O-Vieve looked away. Obviously, the question had disturbed her.

Qui-Gon took the opportunity to press the point. "Adi Gallia and I have seen your Tech Circle and your Med Circle. We have seen what you *do* have compared to what you *could* have. There have been advances in medicine and technology that could save your people suffering and hardship. Is it right to deny them?"

"We do not deny them," V-Tan said, shaking his head. "We save them."

"There must be some sacrifice in order to

preserve the General Good," O-Vieve said, turning back to them. Her voice once again rang with firm authority. "This meeting is over. We will send your Padawans after you. We have a good ship, well-stocked, equipped with a hyperdrive for them. We send you good wishes on your journey." Her blue eyes suddenly held the glint of steel. "But if you try to remain in Kegan atmosphere, know this: Your ship will be blasted out of the sky."

CHAPTER 16

Obi-Wan and Siri were able to slip back into the throng of students crowding around the large data screen while the stragglers completed the course.

O-Bin read the scores, her usual fixed smile on her face. It faltered.

"O-Siri and V-Obi, step forward."

Obi-Wan and Siri stepped forward.

"You have tampered with the data screen," she rapped out. "Ten punishment marks apiece —"

"Excuse me, Guide O-Bin." The soft-spoken girl named O-Iris spoke up. "V-Obi and O-Siri completed the course that fast. I saw them leap up on the durasteel wall."

"And I saw them navigate the twisting beam in only three seconds," another boy said. "No one has ever done that."

"They were already through the first lap

while I was only a third through the first," someone else said.

O-Bin's smile disappeared. She cleared her throat. "I see. Well. Let us see if O-Siri and V-Obi can match their skill on the rec course with obedience in class."

She walked off quickly. The students lined up to follow. Many glanced at Obi-Wan and Siri, speculation in their eyes. Obi-Wan had not foreseen that their prowess on the rec course would gain them more attention. Obviously, no one had ever run the course so fast.

Back in class, O-Bin began the lesson.

"Today we will cover the Kegan system of government as compared to other worlds. After studying other societies throughout the galaxy, V-Tan and O-Vieve have devised the best form of government. No one citizen on Kegan is more important than any other —"

"Really?" Siri said bluntly. "Then why do V-Tan and O-Vieve tell you what to think and what to do?"

"Three marks, O-Siri. You're amassing quite a collection," O-Bin said, her smile tight. "I suppose you enjoy kitchen duty."

"It sure beats sitting in class," Siri shot back.

This time, Obi-Wan heard a few students stifle a giggle.

"Two more marks," O-Bin said. "Getting back to the lesson, the freedoms we enjoy here on Kegan are unparalleled —"

Again, Siri interrupted. "Is that why all the children are confined to a walled compound and can't leave without triggering an alarm?"

"O-Siri!"

"And why aren't citizens free to travel off-planet?" Obi-Wan chimed in.

"V-Obi! Four marks for both of you!"

"But Guide O-Bin, they have a point," O-Iris said. "Can you address it?"

O-Bin's lips thinned. "No, I cannot. It is not a valid observation."

"It seems valid to me," V-Ido said hesitantly.

"And if we're free, why can't we choose what jobs we want to do?" another student asked.

"My father wanted to work in the Tech Circle, but was assigned to Traffic Control," someone said. "He hates it."

"They say they are not of our world," O-Iris said. "You call them liars. Yet we saw how they ran the course. No one on Kegan has that kind of skill."

"That's enough!" O-Bin's face was red. She turned to Siri and Obi-Wan. For once, her anger was evident, not covered up with a bland, false smile. "This is all your fault!" she said shrilly. "Yours is not to question The Learning! It has been devised by those far wiser than you. It is taught by those who know more than you."

"Then you should be able to explain it," Siri pointed out.

"If we are so free, why can't we speak out?" O-Iris asked.

"Enough!" O-Bin shouted. She stabbed at a red button by the door. Seconds later, Security Guides burst in.

She pointed to Obi-Wan and Siri. "Take them away! They have disrupted my class! They are enemies of the General Good!"

Obi-Wan and Siri were pulled out of class and taken to the admin center. There, a stern Control Guide told them that because of their repeated disruptions, they were being reassigned.

Their destination was the Re-Learning Circle.

Obi-Wan and Siri exchanged a glance of satisfaction. It was exactly as they'd hoped.

They were marched across the yard and into the field, then down the ramp into the facility. Immediately, all air and light were blocked out. The Re-Learning Circle was dank and cold, the walls and floors the same shade of dull gray.

They were separated immediately. Obi-Wan was taken to a cell and locked inside. The light was dim. There was a mat on the floor to sleep on. That was all.

He did not know what he had expected. But he had not expected this.

Within minutes, his door hissed open. A Guide in a navy chromasheath tunic and pants walked in, a bundle in his arms.

"I am the Guide who will start you on the path of Re-Learning," he said. "Put this on." He held out a sensory-deprivation suit.

Obi-Wan knew he had to go along for now, until he could find Davi. He climbed into the suit and the Guide fastened it securely. He could not see or hear. The world around him dropped away. He could only hear his own breathing.

A lecture began in the padded earphones that covered his ears. He could not dislodge it no matter how he twisted. It was similar to the blackout hood he had worn at the Temple for the cooperation exercise. The difference was he could not remove this himself. He was trapped.

Kegan is a perfect society dedicated to the General Good. The Guides are here to help you. Do not trust others. Only trust your Guides.

The Inner Core worlds are full of dangers . . .

Travel is difficult and unnecessary . . .

Kegan medicine is the most advanced in the galaxy . . .

"Wrong!" Obi-Wan screamed despairingly. "It's all wrong!"

But he could not block out the voice.

CHAPTER 17

Qui-Gon and Adi entered their transport. Adi took the controls. She coolly eyed their starfighter escorts as she fired up the engines.

"Those are so old they should be junked," she said. "We won't have any problem outrunning them."

"Let's hope those laser cannons are just as old," Qui-Gon remarked mildly.

They rose smoothly and headed for the upper atmosphere, the starfighters flanking them closely. Adi was one of the best Jedi pilots Qui-Gon knew. Her response time was amazingly fast, and her feel for her craft was instinctive. If anyone could lose four starfighters without risking damage to their craft, it was Adi.

Because they knew one thing: They would not leave Kegan without their Padawans.

Qui-Gon had thought Adi too cautious at

times during this mission. Now he saw how determined she could be.

"Ready for a ride?" she asked Qui-Gon.

He checked to make sure he was securely strapped in his seat. "Ready."

With one deft movement, Adi flipped the craft over, nearly clipping the wings of the starfighter next to it. She dived down at a screaming speed, then rolled several times. Trying to keep up, one starfighter spiraled out. The starfighter pilot fought to stabilize his craft.

"That model doesn't have the maneuverability this one does," she murmured. "Pity."

Adi pushed the engines to maximum speed and turned hard right, pushing the ship to the limits of its maneuverability. Warning blaster fire erupted off their port side, but Adi was already turning as she climbed, and it passed harmlessly by the wing. It ripped into the wing of the other starfighter, however. Flames erupted from its fuel line.

"Hoped that would happen," Adi muttered. The second starfighter took off, back down to the planet for repairs.

Now Adi reversed direction. Instead of trying to elude the two remaining ships, she headed straight for them. Thinking she was about to crash into them, both starfighters went into a dive and fired at the same time.

Adi was able to easily avoid the fire with a few quick turns. The starfighters were below them now, still diving. Adi pushed the engines to the maximum. They zoomed off and soon lost the two craft.

"Good flying," Qui-Gon complimented her. "And here I thought Yoda sent you on this mission just to watch over me. Maybe he knew we'd need your flying skills."

Adi threw him an amused glance from her dark, almond-shaped eyes. "Yoda didn't send me to watch you. Not in the way you think. Siri and I are a new team. He wanted her to see how a good Master–Padawan team operates."

"So Yoda isn't keeping an eye on us?"

"On the contrary. You and Obi-Wan have proven your effectiveness. Yoda felt Siri needed to learn cooperation with another Padawan as well."

Qui-Gon considered this. "I believe I learned the same lesson," he said softly.

Adi gave him one of her rare smiles. "And I as well."

Qui-Gon plugged in the coordinates for Kegan's high plateau and they settled back for the short ride. Soon they zoomed over the targeted area. Mist shrouded the landscape below. Qui-Gon peered first at his data screens, then with his own keen gaze. The mist parted, and it appeared — a vast compound ringed with a high stone wall. Long, low-domed buildings lay within the larger compound as well as cultivated fields and open space.

"The mist is a good cover," Adi said. "I'll land outside the wall near those rocks."

They landed, concealing the ship behind a stand of rocks and scrub. They climbed out and quickly crossed a field and scaled the wall.

The mist lay low on the ground, so thick it was hard to see more than a short distance ahead. Qui-Gon and Adi patrolled the compound, letting their keen senses tell them when Guides were near. They moved like shadows through the fog.

They climbed on top of the buildings and looked through the skylights. They peered through every window. They found nothing.

"They aren't here," Adi Gallia said. "Maybe they were, and they moved them. No doubt O-Vieve and V-Tan have already sent out an alert for us. They know we'll head here. I think we should leave and consider our next step. Maybe we should head back to Kegan and see if Melie and Nen have come up with anything."

Qui-Gon paused. He lifted his head and

closed his eyes. He felt the Force around him. He reached out to it, hoping it would tell him if his Padawan was near.

He felt nothing.

"All right," he said reluctantly. "Let's go."

CHAPTER 18

At first he had struggled to block out the voice.

Trust the Guides to show you the way to the General Good. They monitor it. They know it. Trust them. Do not trust your friend or neighbor.

Then he realized that he should not struggle. That only made the voice more insistent. He practiced the Jedi way and accepted. The voice washed over him like water. He did not have to drink it in.

How long would this go on? It seemed to be lasting for hours. He could find his calm center; the voice would not penetrate. He knew Siri could do the same. They would not go crazy listening to that steady, melodic voice that told lie after lie.

But what about Davi?

At last he was released from the sensory-deprivation suit by his Guide. At first he could only blink. The soft noises of people and move-ment outside his door, the breathing of the Guide seemed loud and intrusive. Obi-Wan imagined that this was like being born.

"How long have I been here?" Obi-Wan asked.

"That I cannot say," the Guide said pleas-antly. "Now it is time for the cleansing room. I'll lead you if you can't see quite yet. It's normal."

"I can see." Obi-Wan's eyes were adjusting now. The gray walls and gray floors were like an extension of the darkness he had been plunged into for so many hours.

He walked next to the Guide down the corri-dors, passing a Medic Guide, this one different from the one he'd seen aboveground so many days before.

No. Today. I saw that Medic Guide earlier to-day.

He had to hold on to his sense of time. He would find a way to mark it in his room.

I won't be here that long. We came for Davi. We'll find him and get out.

They had come because they felt they owed Davi. They had come to help a friend. They had thought it would be easy to rescue him and get out. They were wrong. This would not be easy.

It had been impulsive, Obi-Wan realized. And he had promised himself back at the Temple that he would not be impulsive again. He would be careful.

Maybe he'd been influenced by Siri. She was always ready to jump, to move, to take action. He shouldn't have listened to her.

Do not listen to others. Listen only to the Guides.

Obi-Wan shook his head, blocking out the memory of the voice.

The Guide ushered him into the cleansing room. He pointed out the heating spray and cooling spray, towels, and a fresh tunic.

"I will be back in three minutes," he said.

Obi-Wan felt the pulse of the warm water against his back. He felt a sudden connection to the land above him, the living creatures, the beings around him. Qui-Gon was here. He was searching.

He knew it. He felt the strong, sure connection.

I'm here, Qui-Gon. I am below. Don't stop searching.

They had this connection once, but it had frayed. Would Qui-Gon hear him? Would he answer him?

He felt nothing.

Obi-Wan moved to the cooling spray, then toweled himself off and dressed.

He was on his own. He could trust no one.

Only the Guides could be trusted for truth and . . .

Obi-Wan stopped in the middle of buckling his utility belt. He had not heard those words as spoken by the voice in his ear. He had heard the words in his own voice.

Fear snaked through him. They had gotten to him in only one session.

Obi-Wan took a breath. He summoned up his training. He focused on the calmness within. It drove out the fear.

I am not alone, he told himself firmly. *I have Siri. And I trust her.*

CHAPTER 19

Food service took place in a large hall filled with students. Obi-Wan could not see their faces. Like him, they wore concealing hoods. Strict silence was maintained. Security Guides patrolled the aisles between the long tables, making sure no one started a conversation.

The Learning Circle had been strict. Friendships were discouraged. If one student got too close to another, they would find themselves transferred to a different quad. But conversation was allowed at food times, and students did interact.

Here, everything was designed to break a student down. Isolation was the tool.

Obi-Wan tried to peer under hoods to see if Siri was looking for him. He searched for a small, slight form that could be Davi. He could not tell if either of his friends were here.

A harsh buzzer sounded, and there was a

loud scrape of chairs against the floor as every-one stood, finished or not. Obi-Wan lined up with the others. How would he be able to make contact with Siri? He would have to find a way. Perhaps he could fake an illness. There seemed to be many med wards in this building . . .

Ahead of him, his sharp eyes had caught a slight movement. A slender tail flicked out of a tunic pocket. The student quickly put a hand in-side.

Davi!

They marched down the long gray hallway in a row. One by one the students split off into separate cells. Obi-Wan kept his head down but his eyes fixed on Davi. He made a note of the cell Davi had disappeared into. There were no numbers on the doors, so he counted the doors until he got to his own.

He would contact Davi tonight. There was no time to lose. Davi was sensitive. He was afraid of being alone. What was this place doing to him?

And how would he find Siri? Obi-Wan pon-dered the problem. He would have to trust the Force to guide him. He could not delay any longer. He would use his lightsaber to cut through his cell door after lights out.

That night, he timed the regular stroll of the Security Guides. He calculated the distance down the hall. He would have just enough time to get Davi, pause inside his cell for the next patrol, then take off and look for Siri. It would be risky. He would have to count on the Guide to not notice the damaged cell doors. The lighting was low enough that he just might get away with it.

A buzzer announced lights out, and three seconds later his light was extinguished. Obi-Wan sat cross-legged on the floor of his cell. He would wait until he was sure that most students were asleep.

He had waited only a few minutes when a whisper came to him faintly.

"Obi-Wan! What are you doing? Catching a nap?"

"Siri?"

"Who do you think it is, V-Tarz? Stand back."

The glow of molten metal illuminated his room. Siri was cutting a hole in the door with her lightsaber. Obi-Wan sprang forward to help. Soon they'd cut an opening big enough for him to squeeze through.

Siri's bright eyes gleamed at him. "What were you waiting for? Are you starting to like it here?"

By now Obi-Wan was used to her sense of humor. "Come on," he said. "I know where Davi is."

They hurried down the hallway. "I think Qui-Gon is somewhere in the Learning Circle," he said. "I feel it."

"I don't feel anything," Siri said. "But I don't have that kind of connection to Adi yet. Maybe someday we'll work together as well and you and Qui-Gon."

It was a backhanded compliment, but it was the first time she'd acknowledged that Obi-Wan had more experience than she did.

They reached Davi's door. Quickly, they cut a hole and climbed through. Davi rose on his elbows, shocked to see Obi-Wan and Siri climb into his cell.

"What are you doing here?" he whispered. "You'll get us all in trouble."

"It could get worse than this?" Siri asked, waving her lightsaber at the bare cell.

Davi didn't smile. He lowered back onto his sleep mat and curled into a ball. "I'm sure it could," he said. "Go away."

"Davi, you have to come with us," Obi-Wan said urgently.

"You have to trust us," Siri added.

"I only trust the Guides," Davi said. "They show me the way to the General Good. They monitor it. They know it. I trust them."

"That's the voice talking," Obi-Wan said.

"I do not trust my friend or neighbor," Davi

whispered. "I trust the Guides." He looked at them pleadingly. "This is all I know. Please go away."

Siri stepped forward and sat on the floor next to Davi. "There are many things in the galaxy that are good, Davi. If Kegan let in the good things from outside, it would be a better place. Perhaps some of the illnesses you have here are now curable. Like the Toli-X Virus."

Davi rose on his elbows again. "B-but that is incurable. My parents died of it."

"A cure was discovered shortly after the virus began to sweep the galaxy," Siri said gently. "If Kegan had been in touch with the rest of the galaxy, many would have been saved. I'm sorry to tell you this."

"I don't believe you." Davi shook his head back and forth. "The Guides don't lie. The Guides don't lie."

"Davi, why are there so many med facilities here at the Re-Learning Circle?" Obi-Wan asked him.

"Because the children cannot be cured," Davi said. "If they are in sight of others, it is bad for the General Good."

"If an animal was hurt, would you lock it away, or would you try to cure it?" Obi-Wan asked. "This place is wrong, Davi. You must know that."

Davi looked up at them, stricken.

"We are your friends," Siri said urgently. "We would not lie to you. You know that we come from another world. We have seen these things." She stood. "Will you come with us?"

Davi hesitated. Outside in the hall, they heard the footsteps of a guard. Would Davi turn them in?

They heard the footsteps walk by, then fade.

Davi stood. "I'm coming with you."

Obi-Wan and Siri reached out and each put a hand on Davi's forearm. They smiled at each other.

"Wait." Davi looked at them hesitantly. "Can I take Wali?"

Siri and Obi-Wan exchanged a glance. Rescuing someone else would take time and could endanger them. But they couldn't refuse Davi.

They nodded.

Davi squatted by the wall. Carefully, he eased out a stone from the wall. He plucked out a small furry creature and slipped it into his pocket.

"All right. I'm ready."

They moved quietly down the hall. Suddenly, a faint, mewing cry split the silence.

"Davi, you have to make Wali be quiet," Obi-Wan advised him.

"That wasn't Wali," Davi whispered.

They heard the cry again. It was muffled, and Obi-Wan realized now that it came from one of the rooms off the hall. Then he felt it —

"It's a baby," Siri breathed.

"It's O-Lana," Obi-Wan declared.

CHAPTER 20

They were almost to the wall when Qui-Gon felt the surge in the Force. But all he saw was a field of green grain.

"They are here," he said to Adi.

She nodded. "I feel it, too. But where?"

Qui-Gon crouched down. He put his hands on the dirt. He closed his eyes. "Here."

He felt vibrations. Running footsteps.

"We've been spotted," Adi said.

They activated their lightsabers as the Security Guides thundered toward them. The Guides were armed with blasters.

The Guides were not used to skilled opponents. Qui-Gon and Adi used their lightsabers to deflect fire only. Working in perfect tandem, they flanked the guards and spun and evaded while they maneuvered them backward.

A utility shed stood at the edge of the field. Qui-Gon and Adi moved the Guides back toward it, step by step. The Guides stumbled, tried to rally, and fell back.

When they were almost to the shed, Qui-Gon circled around and opened the door. Then he leaped over the Guides to face them again. Together with Adi, he drove them into the shed. Then they closed and locked the door.

"Now what?" Adi Gallia asked. "No doubt they are calling for help on their comlinks."

"We find the way in," Qui-Gon said.

Obi-Wan and Siri quickly cut a hole in the door.

They found themselves in an infirmary. Children and young people lay on sleep couches. Some were hooked up to monitors. Others were attached to tubes. Some of them opened their eyes as the Jedi passed, only to stare at them dully. Obi-Wan wondered if they were given sleep potions.

O-Lana lay in a crib with high sides. Crying softly, she pulled herself to her feet when she saw Obi-Wan and Siri.

"You must not cry, O-Lana," Obi-Wan told her soothingly.

She stopped crying. Then she held out her arms and looked directly at Davi.

After a glance at Obi-Wan and Siri to make

sure it was all right, Davi picked up the child and cradled her against his chest.

"I'll protect her as we go," he promised.

They hurried out of the infirmary and headed for the exit ramp. The next guard patrol was moments away.

But luck wasn't with them. They turned the corner and ran straight into a group of Security Guides about to change shifts.

Surprised, the Guides fumbled for their weapons. Obi-Wan and Siri activated their lightsabers. They glowed in the dim hallway, and the Guides stopped momentarily, even more surprised. They had never seen lightsabers before.

"Stay behind us, Davi," Obi-Wan ordered.

He and Siri moved forward. This time he knew she would not fight for herself. She would fight with him, for all of them.

Blaster fire pinged around them, and their lightsabers met it, a blur of speed and motion. They covered each other and leaped high, dropped to one knee, reversed direction, changed hands, all without pausing. Protecting O-Lana and Davi was their only objective.

An alert sounded. One of the Guides must have activated it. The halls rang with a clanging alarm. Obi-Wan heard footsteps pound behind them. Soon they would be surrounded.

"This way," he called. He pushed Davi and O-Lana gently down an adjacent corridor.

The Guides followed, a mass of bodies in chromasheath armor, blasters firing. The small missiles fired by the beam tubes thudded into the walls around them. The air began to fill with smoke.

Obi-Wan and Siri pressed on. They could see the exit ahead. But Obi-Wan didn't know whether they could protect Davi and O-Lana, continue to fight the Guides, *and* activate the ramp. It would take time to figure out how the ramp was operated. There was most likely some sort of key or code. Their backs would be against a wall. Siri glanced over at him, and he knew she had thought of the same problems ahead.

More Guides suddenly appeared, running down an adjacent corridor. Obi-Wan felt sweat trickle down his back as he deflected a sudden burst of blaster fire. Would the battle end here? Would they have to surrender in order to save O-Lana and Davi?

Just then he heard a *whirr* and a clicking sound. The door slid open. A ramp shot up to the surface and fresh air flooded the hall. A split second later, Qui-Gon and Adi raced down the ramp, their lightsabers activated. With one quick glance they took in the situation, then leaped into the fray.

The Security Guides had gained confidence as their numbers increased. But four Jedi were too much for them. Their blaster fire was deflected back relentlessly. They had to keep diving to the floor or ducking behind carts to avoid it.

Finally, they simply dropped their weapons and ran.

The Jedi turned to one another. The battle was over. Obi-Wan took O-Lana from Davi's arms. He handed her to Qui-Gon.

"I bet you've been searching for this," he said.

Qui-Gon looked over O-Lana's head at him. "I have been searching for you, too, Padawan. I am glad to have found you."

CHAPTER 21

When the citizens of Kegan found out what was happening in the Re-Learning Circle, they revolted. They were horrified that children were hidden away and put in solitary confinement for questioning authority or having a chronic ailment. It violated everything O-Vieve and V-Tan had claimed Kegan valued.

Every citizen packed the Gathering Circle to debate the problem. Qui-Gon, Obi-Wan, Adi, and Siri observed as V-Tan and O-Vieve were voted out as Benevolent Guides. A new council was swiftly appointed. Soon debate raged regarding travel outside Kegan. At last a vote was taken. A majority favored sending an envoy to the Galactic Senate. In the meantime, they would petition the Galactic Senate to send medical and scientific advisors to the planet to bring Kegan up to date.

Soon after, the Learning Circle was closed.

Students returned home to their families. They were given a short vacation until a new schooling system could be set up. People opened their homes to the orphans from the Re-Learning Circle, and the rest returned to their parents.

It was time for the Jedi to leave. They stood with Nen, Melie, and Davi at the landing platform. Melie handed Lana to Siri.

"Nen and I have decided that it is best for Lana to go," she said, tears in her eyes. "I have seen what the Jedi are and what they can do. We must honor her gift."

"O-Vieve and V-Tan were right about many things," Nen said, touching his daughter's cheek. "One of them is that we must sacrifice for the General Good. It is better for Lana, better for the galaxy, if she is able to be taught completely."

"We shall care for her and honor her," Adi Gallia said. "She will grow wise in the ways of the Force, and her life will be one of service."

"I can ask for no better life for my daughter," Melie said.

Nen put his arm around Davi. "And a new child has come into our lives. Davi has agreed to stay with us."

"If he can stay away from the Animal Circle," Melie teased. "Our friend Via works there. She is teaching him how to care for the animals."

"I will never forget you," Davi told Obi-Wan and Siri shyly.

Obi-Wan put his hand on Davi's forearm. "We will always be your friends, Davi."

"If you ever need us, you have only to summon us," Siri told him.

"Safe journey," Nen said. "We are grateful to the Jedi for working to restore our world to justice."

Nen, Melie, and Davi walked away. Siri brought Lana into the ship to settle her in for the journey. Adi went inside to do her last-minute checks.

Obi-Wan took a last look at Kegan from the landing platform. "This world was a puzzle to me," he said. "I still don't understand how an entire planet could place its trust so blindly in visions and dreams."

"I'm not surprised," Qui-Gon said. "All living beings find comfort in a truth that makes their lives easier to bear. Here on Kegan the people did not have the strife or hunger that we've seen on other planets. Why should the people question a system that brought them ease and comfort?"

"But their freedom was an illusion," Obi-Wan argued.

"We do not know if O-Vieve and V-Tan's visions were wrong, Padawan," Qui-Gon said thoughtfully. "O-Vieve's vision of the future was clouded, but that doesn't make it invalid. Perhaps she just misinterpreted what she saw."

"That I don't believe," Obi-Wan said. "I can't imagine one central evil controlling the whole galaxy. That would be impossible."

"I hope we do not see it, Obi-Wan," Qui-Gon said. "But we cannot say it is impossible. Haven't you experienced enough of chance and evil in the galaxy to realize that?"

Obi-Wan shook his head stubbornly. "She saw darkness coming from the Jedi itself. That could never happen."

Sun suddenly burst through the clouds overhead, dazzling Qui-Gon's sight. The glare caused Obi-Wan's features to blur and dissolve. For a moment, Qui-Gon didn't see the boy. He saw an elder man, alone, living on a desolate planet, his only companions his dark memories.

Qui-Gon felt the same shiver he'd experienced in O-Vieve's presence. Did he just have a vision of himself as an elder? Was that the dark vision O-Vieve had seen for him?

Then a sudden truth pierced him. *That isn't me. It is Obi-Wan.*

Or was it?

The sun retreated behind the clouds. The world became clear again. Qui-Gon studied Obi-Wan. He saw the familiar boyish features, the shining eyes. He found reassurance in the sight of his youth. *The future is not fixed, but fluid,* he told himself. Visions did not have to come true.

"Qui-Gon, are you all right?" Obi-Wan asked.

"Perhaps we should not speak of evil and darkness just as we've completed a successful mission," Qui-Gon suggested lightly. "Let us enjoy this moment. Justice has returned to Kegan."

"And if darkness lies ahead of me, I will fight it," Obi-Wan resolved.

Qui-Gon put a hand on his shoulder. "We will fight it together, Padawan."

The Early Adventures of
Obi-Wan Kenobi and Qui-Gon Jinn

STAR WARS

JEDI APPRENTICE

Scholastic Inc., P.O. Box 7502, Jefferson City, MO 65102

Please send me the books I have checked above. I am enclosing $_____ (please add $2.00 to cover shipping and handling). Send check or money order–no cash or C.O.D.s please.

Name_____ Birthdate_____

Address_____

City_____ State/Zip_____

Please allow four to six weeks for delivery. Offer good in U.S.A. only. Sorry, mail orders are not available to residents of Canada. Prices subject to change.

SWA1199

Visit us at www.scholastic.com

The Sky Will Fall.

THE SEVENTH TOWER™

Coming June 5, 2000
A new series from Lucasfilm and the publishers of *Star Wars Jedi Apprentice* and *Animorphs*

www.scholastic.com
www.theseventhtower.com

◣ SCHOLASTIC